IMPULSE

MEGAN STOCKTON

D & T
PUBLISHING

This one's for the girls. If you need an alibi, you were with me all night watching movies. If you need help *moving furniture*, I know a professional.

And to every 'Boss' — I hope you never feel safe. I hope you always look over your shoulder. Most importantly though… I hope you suffer.

"Tell me again just how sorry you are."

— Jennifer Hills, *I Spit on Your Grave*

"It should be them, not us."

— Elizabeth, *What Good Girls Do* (Jonathan Butcher)

IMPULSE

CHAPTER ONE

Jason hated his life.

It wasn't enough to just hate his job anymore. He had been a teacher for almost thirty years now. *Thirty fucking years*. It was hard for him to fathom that he was old enough to have been working that long, let alone that he was in his fifties. He had realized pretty quickly that he'd picked the wrong field of work. He hated kids of any age, but teenagers were a whole different monster. The boys were full of raging hormones and stupid as shit. The girls were just hot enough to tempt you, but obviously *students*.

He'd slipped up a couple of times with some of the girls. Crossed a few lines here and there. Nothing that had ever amounted to anything or had gotten him into any kind of trouble. He figured most of those girls either wouldn't utter a word to anyone out of embarrassment, or they would just brag about the situation to their friends and no adult would ever believe them. It was what it was, and Jason was much more careful these days. It made the job even less enjoyable to know that he had to walk on eggshells. But every four years the kids were brand new, and he could start over and make a few more bad decisions.

It wasn't just the job though. Jason was married to his own high school sweetheart. She had been the prettiest girl in the school, and he'd been a total schmuck. Oh, how the tables had *turned*. A few decades and a couple of kids later and she was fat, tired, and always wore clothes way too big for her. She kept her hair in this frizzy, messy bun and never wore makeup. Sometimes he thinks she put on the weight, and the stained jogging pants and oversized band t-shirts, when she got pregnant with their first kid and *never fucking took any of it off*. Most days, it just pissed him off to look at her.

They had two teenage daughters. Some days he thought he hated them, too. You would think there was some kind of biological mechanism that made it harder for fathers to hate their children. Women had that thing. The thing that kept them from killing their kids, even when they were total assholes. He just didn't have that. He didn't want his daughters to *die*, and he loved them, he thought. They were pretty, got those looks from their mother he supposed. They brought friends over sometimes for sleepovers, pretty girls that wore long t-shirts with no bra and just their underwear around the house. They'd walk into the kitchen to retrieve a bag of popcorn and giggle, calling him *Mister* Burnham. This just reminded him that he was old. He was an old man, and it made him feel dirty when he watched them walk back down the hallway to his daughter's room. It actually caused a little bit of guilt when he snuck around in the middle of the night, or walked by the cracked bathroom door as they brushed their teeth. It made him resent his daughters for being pretty and having pretty friends. It made him furious that someday they would get lazy and depressed and fat and ugly, just like their mother.

Yeah, Jason hated everything about his miserable life.

So, it was no surprise that he found himself parked in front of the overlook at Fallen Church Lake, thinking about mashing the gas and driving over. The car was in park but still running, and he thought about how easy it would be to drive through the wooden barrier and just topple down into the lake below. Drowning would probably be a shitty way to go though, especially in a vehicle. You had time to regret what you did, time to decide you didn't want to die. That's what he didn't need. He needed something quick, something he couldn't back out of when he inevitably chickened out.

He rubbed one out in the car, thinking it might be his last, but found himself reconsidering his decision to kill himself after a little post-nut clarity. Instead, he loaded one of his hookup apps and started scrolling through the faces. He knew by now which girls would agree to meet up with him. This wasn't prostitution (he *wished* he knew how to find a prostitute), and there weren't that many women who were into a man his age. He wasn't young enough, but not quite that silver fox territory either. He tried to cut himself a little slack but he knew he wasn't exactly a ten in the looks department. He had an aggressively receding hairline, more than a beer gut, and he'd never been great looking. Even in his youth, he hadn't turned any heads. His best friend, Jerry, used to say, "Jason, your wife is a saint. Smoking hot girl like she was, marrying some loser like you. Bet she's into charity, huh?"

Jerry's wife was dead though. Lucky Jerry.

A busty redhead's photo showed up next on his carousel of debauchery. She had on thick eye makeup and caked-on foundation, but it was mostly blurred by a filter she'd used. He was sure she was aiming to look like an edgy, younger version of herself... but she mostly resembled a chain smoking, coked-out convenience store clerk. She'd do just fine.

There was a point in his life that he had worried about disease and the consequences of his choices and actions, but those years had long passed. All he looked for now was easy access and no strings attached.

He swiped the 'contact' button. The green dot by her name signaled that she was online, and her profile said she was always ready for a good time. Three dots bounced across the screen as she typed, and he found himself losing patience with how long it took her to formulate the simple response: *Send pic.*

"Fucking dammit...," he muttered.

That was always a red flag for a hookup. No one was looking for *him*, but maybe she just wanted to make sure he was a real guy and not some weirdo. Could you tell from a photo who was going to murder you and use your flesh as a lampshade? What was the difference between the guy next door and Buffalo Bill anyway? He turned on his front facing camera, cringing at his double chins. He lifted the phone up, tilting his face as he gave himself as many angles as possible. He snapped a few and then scrolled through them. Not too shabby, actually.

Jason selected one and sent it over. She didn't respond immediately, and the seconds ticked by after it gave him a notification that she'd viewed the photo. He followed up with: *Just got off work, ready to fuck if you are.*

He had found that sometimes being crass was exactly what these women were after. It made him look desperate, willing to be dragged along, abused, used. That was him. That's what he wanted.

Sent u pin to motel. U pay for room.

It was the address to a motel on the north end of the county, he knew the one. He'd been there a lot recently, it was one of the only places that offered hourly rates... not that Jason ever needed more than an hour. The motel required you to book at least two. That gave him enough time to wash up if the girl left, and he wouldn't have a lingering smell of her on him when he went home. Part of him cared, somehow. When he heard his wife crying into her pillow sometimes, he wanted to roll over and comfort her. When she watched him, when she thought he didn't notice, he wanted to reassure her that everything was alright. But it still wasn't enough to make him want to stop. It wasn't really enough to convince him that he still actually loved her.

He would have to run home first and change clothes, come up with some kind of excuse as to why he needed to go back into work and why he needed to take his wife's car. He hated all of the lies and the excuses, not because of any morality... but because it was so fucking hard to keep up with sometimes.

He backed out of the parking lot and squared up against the highway beside the stop sign. He made eye contact with a young guy in a letterman's jacket as he pulled down the access road, arm slung around a blonde girl in the passenger seat. She was so close to him that she had to have been fucking the gear shifter. Jason was jealous that he'd never had those trips up to the overlook. He hadn't been outgoing or promiscuous in his prime. He had been too worried about being rejected, being judged. He had been too worried about his future.

If only he'd known then what he knew now.

C H A P T E R   T W O

Jason felt suffocated by his home before he ever entered it. As he walked up the sidewalk to the front door, his chest tightened and he thought he could feel a great weight resting on his shoulders. He pushed the front door open, hating the way it grinded against the hardwood floor. It left this grayish trail, a scuff that his wife always scrubbed off the floor before he came home in the evenings. He would never understand why she didn't just leave it there. Every time the door was opened, the floor would become scuffed again. She'd get down on her hands and knees with a bottle of wood oil and a microfiber towel, talking about how you could polish in little circles and it would 'heal' all of the scratches. She had asked him to fix the door before, but he didn't know anything about doors or how to even begin to address the issue. She'd once even ventured as far as to suggest he hire someone. He had other shit he'd rather spend the time and money on.

She was always complaining when he spent money. She seemed to know when he spent a little extra somewhere and didn't tell her. He didn't know how she knew, but he just assumed all women had the propensity to be money-hungry. She would ask him if he'd taken out a new subscription, or mention that she couldn't account for a hundred or so bucks — of course, it was going to hotels and porn subscriptions. He'd joined a few cam sites that were *really* worth the money some nights. It wasn't as good as the real thing, but the girls always acted way more enthusiastic and interested in him. Probably because they were paid to.

His wife's voice came from inside the kitchen, so much joy and warmth that it had to be faked. No one was this happy. No one.

"Hey, sweetheart! I have dinner almost ready…" she trailed off and he could hear the beep of the oven. Once upon a time he had cooked dinner for them. He used to fight to beat her to the kitchen, wanting to let her take a break from her busy day and be pampered. He didn't feel like she had appreciated all the effort he put into her, and now he couldn't stand the idea that he'd ever wasted the time.

"Yeah," he called back, walking slowly towards the sound of her voice. "I'm actually going to have to head back in. Just wanted to stop by to take a quick shower and change into something more comfortable. I've got a ton of tests to grade and I think I'm just going to pull an all-nighter."

She came around the corner to meet him, face drawn in both disappointment and disbelief. He knew she didn't believe him. He didn't blame her. He didn't need her to believe him though, he just needed her to not give a fuck. Her cheeks were blushed pink from cooking over the stove. She always got just a little red-faced when she cooked, even with her hair pulled back and the vent on. He thought he saw a little extra color creeping across her face, maybe anger.

When she finally spoke again, her voice was still fairly calm and collected. "Have you been loading your kids down this semester? Seems like you've had to stay over a lot."

"End of the year, you know how it is. The kids this year are needing all the help they can get to prepare for exams. Just doing what I have to in order to make sure they succeed."

"Well, we can... we can give you space so you can grade them here at home," she insisted. "That way you can have a good dinner that isn't fast food. And you know how bad your back hurts if you don't sleep in the bed."

She said 'we' like the girls would even know if he was home or not. They came straight home and usually went into their rooms. The doors closed and they didn't come out until they were ready for dinner, or ready to go back to school again. *Teenagers.*

"I'm really not hungry."

"What do you mean you're not hungry?"

Jason took a deep breath. "Okay, how about I come home when I'm done? But don't expect me until late. Don't bitch if I come in and wake you up."

"I don't bitch," she responded, indignant and flustered. He thought at first that it was all she was going to say. If he was being honest, she was *never* a bitch. Not unless she had to be. Sometimes Jason wanted to fight with her, just to see a little emotion out of her, a little fire. She was always so happy, so nice, so easygoing. Sometimes he needed something *more*.

"I'll also need to take your car," he added.

"*My* car? Why?"

"I'm on E, and you know I don't have any air conditioning."

It frustrated him that he was the one working his ass off at a job he hated, and she was the one driving a nice car. Any time he met up with girls from the app, he came up with an excuse to take her car. It gave the illusion that he might have a little bit of money. He imagined that girls liked that, although no one ever really commented on what he was driving.

She sniffled, crossing her arms over her chest. "I need it back tomorrow for work. I'm not driving your car again."

He shrugged. "Fine. I'll take a quick shower and be on my way. I'll be back later tonight."

"Jason?"

"Yeah?"

"Be careful. Just be careful, please," she said quietly, wringing the extra length of her black t-shirt.

"Be careful? I'm just going to the school."

She frowned, pursing her lips together. "Right... Okay."

CHAPTER THREE

The further north you went, the darker it seemed to get. The county didn't pay to have any street lamps out here, so the asphalt was the deepest shade of black. It was a starless night too, which just contributed to the density of the late evening. His headlights created an isolated world of visibility, illuminating only the smallest area ahead of him. It wasn't important to see out here though. His wife's car beeped if he crossed any lines, and there wasn't much of anyone else on the road.

The radio droned on sad country songs that all sounded like they were written and sang by the same guy. Something about mama and his dog and the girl that broke his heart. Sometimes they'd throw in whisky and a train. He left it on for the background noise, but otherwise he didn't care for it. He didn't really like *any* music now that he thought about it. His daughters were into some kind of hip hop or R&B, whatever they called that poppy-rap shit these days. His wife was forever a rocker, swooning over the hair bands of the 80s and the grungy greaseballs of the 90s.

The moon illuminated the palest items in the night before he approached them. An old barn, a sign, pieces of garbage left on the side of the road. He thought his eyes were deceiving him when it created a glow in the shape of a human up ahead.

Jason moved his foot off of the gas, gently pressing his toes against the brake at the sight of the figure on the side of the road. For a brief moment, hair raised along his spine. It was like a ghostly apparition that danced along the asphalt. He remembered watching a show about skinwalkers… They usually appeared as animals, but this was still one of those situations where everything reasonable told him he should proceed with caution. He couldn't help but be just the slightest bit curious though.

He leaned forward as his high beams encased her in light then just as quickly as she had appeared he had passed her by. He looked in his rearview, noticing that she had spun around with her thumb jutting out towards the highway. She leaned at the waist, jabbing her hand up and down in the air.

A fucking girl walking down the highway at this hour, in the middle of Bumfuck Nowhere. He pulled off the shoulder of the road, brake lights covering her in a red glow as she approached.

"What the fuck are you doing, Jason?" he muttered to himself as he watched her in the mirror, heart pounding in his chest at first from his fear and apprehension, then from a little element of... *excitement*.

She grew larger in the mirror as she jogged back towards his car, features becoming more clear. She was young. *Really* young. Jason told himself she could be in her twenties, but really he wouldn't have been surprised if she was even younger. But he wished she was just a few months older... Somehow 'legal' made immoral easier to swallow. He was trying to stay on the side of legal. He had a coworker that had gotten busted for venturing a little too close to that line, and even if there hadn't been an official case against him his life was still over. No one wanted him teaching, no one wanted him at church, no one wanted to be associated with him at all... Because he was the fifty-something math teacher that pursued a freshly-eighteen graduate.

She walked like she might have been hurt, but he soon realized she was barefooted as she walked along the still-hot pavement. She was wearing shorts that barely covered her ass, and a dirty tank top. He hadn't passed a house in miles... Where did she come from?

She approached the passenger window, nipples visible through the thin white fabric of her shirt. She leaned down, nose scrunched as she squinted into the dark cab. She had freckled cheeks and shaggy, strawberry-blonde hair that looked like it was probably cut off with a pair of dull scissors in somebody's kitchen. The ends were jagged and frizzled and looked like they had the texture of a straw broom.

"Need a ride?" he asked, smiling at her as he forced his eyes onto her face, it felt like they dragged up with a heavy weight attached to them. The universe had delivered him this prime piece of ass, and he'd be damned if he wasn't at least going to give a little chase.

"You a creep? You look like a fucking creep," she asked, sneering through the words. Her accent was heavy, deep southern. There were a few pockets in the neighboring counties where people talked like this. Some kind of lost language preserved in isolated communities.

"Am I what?"

Jason waded through her thick accent, realizing what she said a fraction of a second before she repeated, "*Are you a creep?*"

"No," he responded, surprised at how unconfident he sounded. He scoffed, shifting uncomfortably in his seat. "No, of course not."

She stared at him for a few moments, chewing on her lower lip. He could see the distrust and uncertainty in her eyes. He supposed if you were going to hitchhike in the middle of nowhere, in the dark, you had to be a little suspicious of strangers. *Anyone* could pick you up. Jason felt a little excitement at the prospect of being dangerous, of being perceived as a threat.

"Alright," she drawled, pulling on the door handle and seating herself next to him. He tried to hide his surprise, but found himself muttering 'okay' and shifting in his seat again.

As she climbed inside and the dome light briefly blinked on, he realized that she wasn't wearing shorts… she was in a pair of underwear. She shoved her dirty feet up on his dash immediately, toes sticking against the humid windshield and leaving ghostly auras. He wanted to ask her not to do that because his wife would throw a fit if the interior of this car was dirty when he got home. He supposed he could stop and grab some wipes on the way back. He didn't want to call her out as soon as she'd gotten in. The car wasn't even in motion yet.

"Where are you headed?" he asked, pulling back out onto the road and being sure to pick up speed. She couldn't go anywhere now. She was here, she was with him.

"Just needin' to get north a little ways… outta the county and you can drop me off."

"I don't plan on going out of the county but I can drop you off along the way."

"Where you goin'?"

"Just… a motel. There's a motel."

"A motel. You *are* a creep. Drivin' a big fancy car like this, then stayin' in some cheapass motel. I know what you're doin', Mr. Bigshot. You're married too, ain'tchya'?"

"I'm not…"

"You need to take your ring off sooner, you can still see the marks on your finger."

He glanced down at his ring finger. She was right, of course. As he'd gotten older his fingers had not only gotten fatter, but they'd started swelling from sitting at a desk all day. Whenever he took off his wedding ring there were little indentations where it had always dutifully sat, and the skin was always a shade paler than the rest of his hand.

The song on the radio ended and the radio hosts started talking about last night's game and a possible killer all in the same breath. *How about that defense? Have you heard about the hitchhiking serial killer? They say he is on the prowl… Who do you think will make it to the playoffs?*

Jason took the opportunity to change the subject, motioning to the radio as he smiled. "Good thing I picked you up. There's a killer on the roads. He could've gotten you."

The girl looked at him out of the corner of her eye, lips twisting into a look of disgust. "Sure, Boss."

She reached over and flipped the radio off and shivered. "How do I know you ain't him?"

Jason didn't respond as he looked over at her again. Something there that was a little experienced, street-smart. Despite the way that she kept an edge towards him, the way that she knew his intentions were not all pure, she wasn't afraid of him. He didn't think he liked it.

She suddenly looked over at him, snaking her head around to look at him straight on. He turned away from her so quickly that he jerked the wheel of the car. She unbuckled and sat cross legged in the seat, facing him.

"You wanna fuck me?"

Jason's stomach sank and he felt his cheeks grow warm. "What the... No. What the hell is wrong with you, kid?"

"I see the way you're lookin' at me," she said, and he heard a tongue ring click against the back of her teeth. "So, tell me how you wanna do it."

Jason felt like his face was on fire, the surface of his eyes even stung with heat. He shook his head at her. "You're too young for me... This is wrong."

"Only if someone finds out, right, *daddy?*"

"Jesus Christ. I'm dropping you off. Get the ..." He stole a glance over at her, and noticed that she was bleeding onto the pale leather of the passenger seat. A dark red oozed from beneath her, staining her white underwear and leaving a smear on the fabric.

"What the fuck? You're... I think you're on your..." He motioned to her, suddenly repulsed. His wife would *murder* him. Thank God it was leather. He wondered if the threads of the seams would retain the odor and stain of her blood. What if this girl was missing or kidnapped or wound up dead? What if the hitchhiking serial killer got her, and then they ended up finding the blood in his wife's car? That was irrational, that was unlikely. He needed to stop thinking of things that were so outlandish...

And then the girl did something that had him reevaluating it all.

She reached down between her legs, propping both feet up onto the dash as she spread her knees apart. He thought he saw her hand disappear all the way to the wrist and he became lightheaded.

"Hey, kid, what the fuck are you doing? Hey, stop doing that. I said *stop it*, dammit! I will kick you out of this fucking car."

The girl pulled out a knife. It was encased in a black sheath, but was sizable. How the fuck did she fit that in there? It certainly explained why she was walking funny down the highway. Her fingers stuck to the tacky fluids that coated the exterior of the weapon, leaving gossamer strands of mucus between her flesh and the nylon sheath as she peeled it away from the blade. It shined silver inside the cab, and as she leaned towards him Jason lifted his foot off of the gas.

"If you slow down, I'm gonna kill you," she said, the slightest chuckle forming at the end of her sentence.

"What the fuck… What the *actual fuck*. You can't be serious. Do you want money? I've got money. "

She reached over, sliding the knife across his thigh. He felt the crawling sensation of panic creep across his flesh, and he was pretty sure his balls had retreated into his abdomen in terror. She reached up in an instant, grabbing his shirt collar and leaning back against the steering wheel so firmly that the horn droned. She smashed her lips against his: the flavor of blood and weed flooding his mouth. She smelled like sweat and motor grease or hot rubber, like a car garage.

She pulled her head away from him, a crooked smile on her lips. Then she smashed her head into his. He heard the pop of their skulls collide. Delirium overtook him, and she grinned at him like she was reeling from the experience in a completely different way. A thick globule of blood oozed from her left nostril and she released a low giggle. She turned the knife blade down and drove it into the annex of his trunk and thigh, he felt it rip through tissue and tendon. Then she elbowed him in the face.

As he lost consciousness, the last thing he remembered was the sound of the engine revving under his foot, and the sensation of the car leaving the road.

C H A P T E R   F O U R

Jason awoke groggily, feeling a dull ache in the center of his shoulders first. His body felt heavy, and first attempts at any motion were useless. He felt like he was on a boat: gently swaying back and forth, a swimming feeling that sent his brain spinning and tied his gut into nauseous knots.

He slowly cracked his eyes open and his skull was immediately flooded with pain. The entirety of his brain was washed in a splash of white-hot agony. He quickly clamped his lids shut, choking as his surprised gasp was cut off by the sensation of a dry cloth between his teeth and across the top of his tongue. He took ragged breaths out of his nostrils, swallowing the scent of blood that was there as it traveled down the back of his throat. The metallic tang elicited the smallest spray of saliva from beneath his tongue which reduced his desire to vomit against the feeling of cottonmouth.

With great deliberation, he forced his eyes open again, this time with more care and hesitation. He noted that he couldn't feel his hands, fingers burning with pins and needles. As his pupils adjusted to the bright stream of light from a window, he was able to finally orient himself.

He was hanging by his wrists, which explained the ache in his back and numbness in his hands. He was gently swinging, toes dangling just above the ground. He realized if he pointed them, he could just barely rest the ball of his foot on the concrete floor, giving him a brief moment of agonizing relief. His calves ached; warmth and the tingle of mobility returned to his fingertips. His shoulders still hurt, but it was slowly improving. He turned his head to the right, noticing first a simple white door: one like you would see in any average American bathroom. Turning his head then to his left, he confirmed that the room was indeed a bathroom… Well, of some kind anyway.

The floor was bare concrete with a silver drain in the depressed middle. There was a claw foot tub underneath a small window, which was fogged with neglect but still had enough visibility that he could see a yard and a gravel driveway that disappeared out of sight in the distance.

He groaned, trying to scream for help but only releasing a husky bray.

He disengaged from observation, suddenly remembering everything that had happened before he got here. The girl on the side of the road, the knife, the car crash. His wife was going to kill him if the car was totaled. Where was the girl? There was no way she would have survived if there had been an accident, she was unbuckled, hanging across him in the driver's seat.

Then he realized it was *daylight* which meant he'd been unconscious at least overnight. Jesus Christ, what was he doing here?

He heard voices on the other side of the door, and craned his neck expectantly. It was a woman's voice, maybe two. He couldn't tell for sure. The voices lowered in tone as they approached the door and he could see shadows just underneath. The sound of a metal key sliding into the lock on the other side echoed in the bathroom, and then the knob turned and the door gently swung open.

The girl from the car was standing there and she was alone. She stepped inside the room and shut the door, leaning against it with her hands tucked together behind her back. She looked more put together than she had in the car. Her hair was washed and the uneven cut now took the shape of a more stylish shag, the dry ends smoothed and hydrated. She wore some makeup on her face, failing to cover a bruise on her forehead and one under her eye, but obscuring the freckles he'd noticed before.

"Hey, Boss. How you feelin'?" she asked, voice the same gravelly rasp that he remembered.

He tried to say something, but any movement of his tongue against the dry cloth nearly sent him retching.

"Let me get that for ya'," she said, reaching up to hook her finger around the rag. She pulled it out of his mouth and he gasped in relief.

"Water, please," he croaked. "Please, I need something to drink."

"Oh, sure. No problemo. I can get you a little somethin'... but first... don't you wanna know what you're doin' here? Don't you wanna know where you are?"

She seemed a little disappointed, leaning towards him with her lips just slightly parted. She had the mildest overbite, just a tiny bit bucktoothed.

"Yeah.... yeah," he whispered, voice cracking.

She smiled at him, eyes lighting up as she walked back to the door. "I'll be right back with a little somethin' for you to drink. Then there's somebody I want you to meet."

When the girl left the room, a cold sweat started pouring down Jason's neck. He didn't know what she was up to, but he knew it couldn't be good. How had she gotten him in here? There was no way a little girl her size could have hauled him up out of his car and into this house. There was no way she hoisted him up to hang him from the ceiling either. She had help. She had accomplices.

Maybe it was some kind of elaborate prank, a joke. He'd pissed off plenty of people in his life, maybe this was somebody's way of getting back at him.

The girl came back inside, but this time left the door behind her standing open. The hallway didn't betray anything about the rest of the house he was in. It was simple wood panel walls, the kind that was popular back in the 70's. The floor was covered in a short berber carpet.

"Here ya' go," she said, holding a glass with a straw to his face. He struggled at first to capture the straw between his lips, and then sucked down half of the liquid with his eyes closed. It was lukewarm water, and had the slightest metallic tinge. Well water maybe, or old pipes. He wasn't going to complain though.

"So I'm not gonna beat around the bush or nothin'," she started, sitting on the edge of the tub and leaning over to rest her elbows on her knees. "We've got you here for... well, let's just call it a game, alright? We got a game we like to play, and sometimes we gotta bring in new things to play with. You know what I mean, don't ya? I know you do. That's why you were out there on them roads, stepping out on your wife and all that. Sometimes you gotta get some fresh meat."

"What the hell are you talking about?" Jason asked, guts tying themselves into nervous knots. "What kind of game are you talking about? This is illegal... you can't keep me here like this. I haven't done anything wrong."

"Oh, you've done plenty wrong... but we ain't talkin' about that, are we? We're talkin' about our game. We want you to play with us and, honestly, you ain't really gotta say."

"Who is we? Who is here with you?"

"I can't tell you that part yet," she said with a grin, winking at him. "The problem is, though..."

She got up and walked over to him, dragging a finger down the center of his chest. He tried to recoil from her touch, but he was unable to do more than swing his legs. He thought about kicking her, just knocking the shit out of her as hard as he could... but he didn't know what good that would do him yet. As of right now, without her he had no way out of here.

She went on, repeating, "The problem is you're just too strong right now for us to handle. It's gotta be fair. Even the playing field. I ain't never been very big, but you don't gotta be strong to win the game. We know you won't play fair though if you get the chance, so we gotta make sure you don't got a choice."

The girl walked back to the door and stepped just around the corner to the right. She pushed in a man in a wheelchair, and sat him facing Jason. If he wanted to, Jason could have reached out and touched him with his toes. The man looked like he might have been middle-aged, but now it was hard to tell. His head and face were shaved sloppily, patches of hair growing rogue across the tanned surface of his skin and scalp. His mouth hung open, drool dripping from his lips. Jason noticed that he was missing most of his teeth on the bottom, but the ones that remained looked to be in remarkably good health. They were white and unblemished. He was wearing a pair of scrub pants, or something similar, and no shirt. He was thin, skin hanging over his bones like the fabric of a collapsed tent.

"This here... this is Mister Sugarman," the girl said enthusiastically with a smile. "Say hello, Sugarman."

Sugarman didn't respond. His eyes didn't move up to Jason, his face didn't react to the girl's words. He just stared, chin resting on his own chest as it rose and fell with calm breath.

"Oh, he's a little shy sometimes but ain't he just the sweetest?" She kissed his cheek. "That's why we call him Sugarman. You could learn a lot from him, so we figured he could stay in here with you for a while. We feel like he's got a lot left to teach somebody."

"What's wrong with him?" Jason asked, voice low. He hadn't expected to sound so calm. There was something eerie about the expression on Sugarman's face. It was almost as though there was nobody home. Like he had checked out a long time ago. What had happened to him? Had the girl and her friends done it?

She looked down at Sugarman, puzzled. "Whatcha' mean?"

"Listen to me, you crazy little bitch," Jason snapped, jerking towards her as much as he could. He propelled himself forward on the tips of his toes.

She snorted in laughter. "You look like a damn ballerina, you know that? What exactly you think you're gonna accomplish threatenin' me, Boss? You think being disrespectful and callin' me names is gonna make me be any nicer to you?"

"I don't really care what you think. Let me down from here right now or..." Jason faltered. Or what? *Or what?* He had difficulty grasping the magnitude of his situation. How serious was this? Was it a joke or not? Things like this didn't happen in real life. Things like this didn't happen to people like him. Good people.

"Yanno," she said, propping her hands on her hips. "I think I'm just gonna give y'all a little time to get to know each other. Then I'll pop back in and see how you're feelin' about everything. But I'm gonna want an apology. Sugarman, you keep an eye on this creep."

She patted Sugarman's thin leg, the motion causing the fabric of his pants to move and give Jason a glimpse of just how emaciated he was.

As she approached the door again, she jabbed a finger in his direction. "Nobody calls me a bitch."

"What's your name then?" Jason asked, desperate to keep her inside the room for just a moment longer. Something about being left alone with the mute Sugarman unnerved him even more than being in a room with the little psychopathic girl.

"You can just call me Baby."

C H A P T E R   F I V E

The moment Baby left, Jason started trying to think of a way to escape. He no longer had any hope that this was some kind of elaborate, albeit innocent, ruse. He wasn't going to waste time waiting around. He couldn't turn himself all the way around, but there was a full length mirror on the opposite wall that gave him a decent glimpse at what was behind him. He could see a sink with a metal medicine cabinet above it, a rack of gray towels, a laundry basket, and a little metal door. It almost looked like a mail slot, but it had a handle.

He looked up at his bound hands, noting that they were bondage-style cuffs: leather with wool padding lining the inside. He twisted his hands around, hoping that he might be able to find enough wiggle room to slide his hands free, but they were fastened tight. They were hanging from two eye hooks on the ceiling, and no matter how hard he bounced, they seemed to hold fast. The room was oddly proportioned, with ceilings higher than normal, but not too high. Has this room been built specifically for this purpose? He shuddered to think of the possibility.

The only other thing in the room was the man in the wheelchair in front of him. He still hadn't moved, just sat there staring off into space with his hands folded neatly in his lap. Judging by the excess skin, Jason thought that maybe he had once had some meat on his bones.

"Hey, man," Jason whispered to Sugarman. "You alright? It's just me and you… it's safe to talk now if you need to say something. Shit, man. What did they do to you? What's your real name?"

Sugarman didn't respond.

Jason pointed his toes on his right foot, balancing himself as he reached out with his left foot to tap Sugarman on the knee. There was still no response. Not a twitch, not a blink, nothing.

"Hey," Jason said again, this time much louder. "Come on, brother. I want to get you out of here. If you could just... if you could stand up or something. Just..."

Suddenly Jason had an idea.

"I'm going to move you, alright?"

He didn't even know if Sugarman knew where he was, let alone that Jason was talking to him. He reached out with his left foot again, stretching as far as he could as he reached for the armrest of the wheelchair. A cramp threatened to take over, a tightness starting in the arch of his foot, but he finally got his big toe laid across the edge of the armrest. The wheelchair rocked slightly, rolling forward just a tiny bit, and then back. This was good: the wheels were unlocked and he could possibly scoot it towards him.

"Come on..." Jason willed, leaning forward to grab the chair again. This time it rolled a little closer, and he was able to grasp a larger area with his foot. He pulled it towards him again, hoping that if he could draw the chair close enough, he could stand on it to give him more access to the ceiling. Maybe he could figure out a way to undo his hands, or pull out the hooks from the ceiling.

He pulled the chair with his foot again, this time more forcefully. The chair came forward a great deal, but instead of moving straight, it turned to the side, spinning around until it was facing the complete opposite direction.

That was when Jason realized that there was a hole in the back of Sugarman's skull.

It wasn't a neat little hole. It was the diameter of a half-dollar and cut through the bone and all. Where Jason assumed brain tissue should be, there was nothing but a massive, black clot. It seemed to pulse, breath, pushing in and out with Sugarman's heartbeat. Jason gagged, trying to turn away but unable to. His stomach turned again and he clamped his eyes shut, body lurching as he vomited. The warm void spilled down his chin and chest, and he nearly choked on it, trying to dip his head down to expel as much of it onto the floor as possible.

"Oh, God, somebody help me!" Jason screamed. "Anybody!

Please!"

He coughed, a chunk of pink barf flying out and landing on the surface of the white tub. He wished he could brush his teeth and take another drink of the water. He didn't care how warm it was, or how putrid it tasted.

Jason couldn't stand to look at Sugarman's mangled skull any more. He tried to spin the chair back around, pushing with all of his might, swinging forward to push with both feet. He grabbed the back with his toes, and pulled... and Sugarman tumbled onto the floor. His head hit the concrete with a loud crack, and the wheels of the chair made little whirring sounds in the air. It reminded Jason of bicycle tires and the noise they'd make when they spun.

"Help! Please!" Jason screamed again, the room filling with echoes in response.

Suddenly the door opened again, and Baby rushed inside. She gasped at the sight of Sugarman on the floor, quickly sitting his chair upright. She locked the wheels and bent down to put her hands under his arms, pulling him up with a grunt. He couldn't have weighed a hundred pounds, but she struggled to get him into the seat. By the time she got him situated, folding his hands back where they were, making sure his pants were straight on his hips, she was panting.

"I am so sorry, Sugarman, sweet baby doll. I shouldn't have put you so close to him. That was my fault and I take full responsibility," Baby cooed, stroking the backs of her fingers across Sugarman's face.

She turned around to glare at Jason, standing up to her full five feet with her fists at her sides.

"You'll pay for that one. Just you wait."

Jason snarled, spitting a wad of vomit-tinged phlegm at her. The loogie hit her in the face, making an audible spatter against her cheek.

Baby's eyes clamped shut, long lashes fluttering as she wiped away the sticky fluid and slung it to the floor. She looked up at Jason with a venomous glare and then shrugged her shoulders.

"If that's the way it's gonna be," she said, and she laughed.

Jason rocked backwards on his toes, legs quivering as he

struggled to steady himself. He thought his left shoulder was going to dislocate. It had gone completely numb again, no matter how much he tried to wiggle his fingers or lean onto the opposite arm he could not regain the sensation.

"I'll be back in a bit, Sugarman," Baby whispered, then turned to look at Jason again. "You done lost your dinner rights, Boss. I don't think that's enough to teach you a lesson though. You seem like you'd be a real thick headed son-of-a-bitch. Might need a little somethin' more to learn not to spit in a lady's face, mightn't ya'?"

Jason swallowed back any pride that he had. He needed to be smart about this. Begging wasn't going to work, being violent wasn't going to work. Making *friends* might... and Sugarman wasn't going to be the friend he needed.

"Listen, I'm sorry," he insisted, trying to sound sincere and not desperate. "I'm just really hungry and thirsty and tired... My arms hurt, really bad. If you could just let me go. Tie me up somewhere else."

"I'm gonna stop you right there. You're gonna get your punishment for callin' me a bitch, for spittin' in my face, for knocking Mister Sugarman down. Then we'll see about startin' you off with a clean slate. Until then... until then you just sit tight and don't go nowhere, alright?"

She giggled and winked at him, seeming proud of her own joke.

Jason waited until she was out of the room and a good ways down the hallway before he let out a frustrated scream, bouncing against the restraints as he thrashed and kicked. Sugarman was out of reach now, still sitting and staring off into space. Somewhere far away from this hellhole, he assumed.

He struggled onto his tiptoes again, squinting at the window now that the sun had retreated somewhere beneath the horizon. He could make out the gravel driveway, but it looked like it disappeared into the distance and he could see nothing except trees and fields. No signs of the highway or any other houses. He could see the edge of a vehicle, just barely in his line of vision. He almost thought it looked like it could've been his wife's car. He didn't remember a crash, an impact. He couldn't remember anything much beyond the girl hitting him in the head with her elbow and spinning around to grab the wheel, grinding her ass against the blade in his crotch.

He had been *stabbed*. He looked down at his legs, struggling to see his groin over his stomach. Why didn't it hurt? Had he imagined the knife being embedded there in the soft spot between his thigh and his trunk? No. It was real. It had happened. He thought now if he pulled the leg up high enough, he could feel the slightest twinge of discomfort.

There were voices in the hallway again, and Jason was *sure* it was two women this time. He listened carefully as their voices got closer, until the door came open again. Baby wasn't alone this time. There was another girl with her: tall, flat chested, athletic. She had dark, curly hair, and the palest brown eyes. Both girls carried cups in their hands: Baby's had a spoon, and the other girl's had a straw.

Baby went straight to Sugarman, getting onto her knees and scooping a spoonful of some kind of gruel into his mouth. To Jason's surprise, Sugarman's sagging lips closed around the spoon and he swallowed every spoonful offered to him. Baby made small 'mmm' noises in her throat as she praised him.

The other girl came to stand in front of Jason, holding up the bowl and straw for Jason. He watched her hesitantly. "I'm not thirsty."

The girl looked over at Baby who huffed, "Sassy, he said he was thirsty. You just told me you was thirsty," Baby insisted, glaring at him.

Sassy reached up higher. "Open your mouth."

Her accent was less obvious, but still undoubtedly from the same area as Baby. Now that she was closer, he saw that she was also freckled, and he thought he might be able to detect some family similarities between the pair of them aside from their totally different hair. She was very calm, almost terrifyingly so. Jason caught himself caught up in her predatory stare, the way that despite all of the softness of her features, he was *afraid* to disobey.

He put his lips around the straw, taking a long drink of the water. He choked, coughing against the burning sensation in his mouth, throat, and nose. His head swam.

"What… the fuck…" he gasped.

"Drink it," Sassy insisted.

"What the fuck is it? It burns."

Jason found tears running down his face, nose afire with every breath.

Sassy leaned in towards him, still a solid foot lower than direct eye level. She locked eyes with him. Truly locked on, had him in a vice grip that he could not look away from.

She spoke again, voice quiet, "Drink it all, and I'll let you down. Scout's honor."

Did he have a choice? His gut was churning and bubbling, he thought he would have to vomit again. He didn't know what it was that she was making him drink, but he knew it wasn't for his health.

"It *burns*," he snarled desperately, gritting his teeth.

"If you don't drink it, I'll funnel it up your ass."

Despite Sassy's dead-serious visage, Baby snickered behind her.

"You better listen to Sassafras," Baby chided. "She means business, don't she, Shugs?"

Jason had never felt so helpless. He knew now that he didn't have a choice. He needed to comply, he needed to submit in every way he could until he had an opportunity to escape or fight back. He nodded his head slowly at Sassy, leaning his head down as far as it would allow, retrieving the straw between his teeth and gulping until the lack of liquid made a rocky crackle at the other end.

"Good boy," Baby whispered, winking at him as she bit her lower lip and grinned.

The room was swimming around him now, but he couldn't tell if it was from the intense nausea or if he had been drugged. His head felt so heavy, falling forward to roll against his chest. It was hard to breathe, and he used all of his strength to pull his impossibly leaden skull backwards. It then lolled back, eyes rolling against his will.

He tried to speak, to say anything at all. All he could mutter was, "God, please… Help me."

He lifted one eyelid, noticing that the girls had left at some point and were now reentering with a ladder. This could be his chance, if he could just get it together. *Pull it together, Jason. Come on.* But the world continued to spiral, pulsing and wriggling beneath the surface, a fluttering cloth atop reality.

Jason thought that he saw Sugarman look up at him, and wink one of his sunken eyes.

CHAPTER SIX

"Wakey, wakey."

Baby's gruff voice echoed around his aching head. He was freezing and he had the strangest lingering sweetness on his tongue. When he opened his eyes, he saw Baby looking down over him. She smiled, clapping her hands. Jason tried to sit up, but found himself unable to do so. He was strapped down again, this time flat against a platform on the floor. He suddenly felt claustrophobic, like his chest couldn't expand beneath the straps to give him enough air.

"He's awake, Sass."

"I can't breathe…"

"You're fine," Baby said, sitting up and rolling her eyes.

He looked down towards his feet where Sassy was approaching and noticed that he was naked. He looked intact… Nothing was missing, or 'vandalized.' He noted that the stab wound on his thigh was sewn up with black suture, but looked neat and healthy other than a rim of the faintest pink. Sassy must have noticed his terror, the color draining from his face, because she paused with the white cloth in her hand and smirked.

"Don't flatter yourself."

Baby interjected, "We only took your pants off 'cause you shit 'em. Not exactly what you were hopin' for when you picked me up, is it?"

"Is this some kind of punishment for being a good guy?" Jason asked, resting his head back down on the floor as he tried to keep from losing his nerve again.

Baby laughed.

"I'm a nice guy," Jason insisted. "I'm a *nice guy*. You were walking on the road, alone, vulnerable. You were lucky. Anyone could have picked you up."

"But *you* picked her up," Sassy said quietly, unfolding the cloth she had been carrying. He noticed that it was fairly thin, maybe a cheese cloth of some kind. "You picked her up. You didn't have the best intentions, did you, Boss?"

"Please don't call me that…"

"Why not, *Boss*?" Baby snickered.

They didn't know, of course, but the nickname had some significance to him. What were the odds? During one of those little 'mistakes' he'd made with one of his students, he had asked the girl to call him 'Boss.' He didn't know why he did it. He'd started with sir, and then professor… master seemed a little pretentious… but 'Boss' landed somewhere in between. Was this his own personal purgatory for that specific sin?

"What would you rather us call you?" Baby asked coyly. "Shitstain?"

The two girls laughed, and Jason did not. He'd rather be called anything.

"My name is Jason."

"We don't care," Sassy confirmed, walking over and draping the cloth over his face. He could barely make out their bodies as dark figures, and he tried to shake the cloth off of his face by slinging his head side-to-side.

"What are you doing?" he asked, feeling panic spike in his chest.

"I told ya'," Baby said, voice rising in pitch. "Nobody calls me a bitch."

"What are you going to do?"

"Ever heard of waterboarding?" Sassy asked.

Jason's heart lurched. He'd heard of waterboarding, but only in regards to prisoners of war. Torture methods. He didn't even remember exactly what it entailed; he just knew it was supposed to be

MEGAN STOCKTON | 37

incredibly inhumane. But it wouldn't *kill* him. He could handle it... He had to handle it.

"I said I was sorry!" he responded in desperation. "I said I was sorry. I got ahead of myself, I panicked."

"Too late for that, you also spit in her face, didn't you?" Sassy asked.

"That he did," Baby said. "But we decided you ain't worth the water so..."

Suddenly, something warm poured over the cloth. Jason hadn't been prepared, he gasped against his own will and his lungs and nose filled with liquid. He coughed and choked, lungs burning as he gasped for air. The salty, bitter fluid made him sick and stung his eyes, pouring in waves down the sides of his face and pooling in his ears. Even when they stopped pouring, it was as though he couldn't pull in enough oxygen through the dampened cloth.

And then they poured again.

He started shaking all over, his entire body quaking and wracked with violent convulsions. He thought his throat was closing up, and he tried to tell himself that it would be over soon. They weren't going to kill him. They were torturing him, they were punishing him. This would end, this would end, this would...

They paused their pouring again and peeled the cloth off of his face. He felt like he had breached a surface, but still could not properly inhale. His lungs were filled with too much... The smell suddenly flooded him.

It was piss. It was fucking piss.

"How you feelin'?" Baby asked, ball of her tongue ring pinched against her front teeth as she smiled at him.

Jason tried to answer her, shaking his head back and forth. Sassy moved to tilt the board he was on, propping it up with what was either a sandbag or a pillow. It allowed the inhaled urine to pour out of his mouth and nose in a frothy purge. He blew the snotty, bloody ammonia out of his nose and coughed as hard as his body would allow.

"He ain't answering, think he needs a few more pours?" Baby

suggested, reaching back down for the yellow-stained cloth again.

"No!" Jason screamed, voice rising to a pitch he'd never used before. "No, I'm sorry. You aren't a bitch. I am so sorry I spit on you. I am… I am so sorry."

"I dunno," Sassy said, exhaling a sigh. "I don't think he sounds sorry. Not really."

"I am," Jason whispered, suppressing a sob. "I am, truly, sincerely."

"Aw, let's cut him a little slack," Baby said, pouting at him. "I think he means it. You willin' to prove you mean it, Boss?"

Jason nodded eagerly. "Yes… Yes. Anything. I'll do anything."

"*Anything?*"

"You ever done shots?" Sassy asked, walking over to a small countertop. He noticed for the first time that this room may have been another bathroom of some kind, but it wasn't the same room as before. It had a similar floor: concrete with a drain, but he could see chipped pieces of old tile piled in the corners. Recent construction or remodel, perhaps?

"Of course I've done shots," he responded, feeling a wave of relief.

"Bet you've never done one of these," Baby said, hand over her mouth as she suppressed a laugh.

Sassy settled down on the ground beside him, holding a shot glass about half full of something viscous. It was whitish yellow, thick and milky. It had partially separated into a clear, mucoid layer beneath.

"What… is that?" Jason whispered. He had his theories. He certainly knew what it looked like, but there was no way… No way. Oh, but there was a way. He'd just been waterboarded with piss, that was *definitely* a shot of jizz.

Baby giggled, putting her hands under her chin. "Sugarman special."

Jason had this confused reaction: a jolt of laughter, while his stomach felt like it fell straight through his ass at the same time. He leaned forward against the restraints, shaking his head from side-to-side.

"You can't do that to me," he insisted.

Baby covered her mouth to hide a giggle, eyes darting to Sassy. She was much less amused, watching him with a calm demeanor. She leaned down towards him — her breath was pleasantly minty in the cloud of ammonia that surrounded him.

"You know, I wanted to make you suck his dick but Baby wouldn't let me," Sassy said quietly, sepia-colored eyes as cool and dense as ice. "If you don't take this like a good boy, I have a much worse plan in mind. Trust me when I say I can be quite creative."

Jason's instinct was to be firm and forceful: to threaten. He had never been in a situation like this before, but in *real life* he would never let anyone do shit like this to him. Especially not two stupid, redneck bitches like this pair. He had always had control. Control of grades, finances, social situations. He'd always had the edge of being older, more experienced, more trusted, more believable.

Then Jason had to remind himself that this *was* real life. This was his reality right now. His next instinct was to bargain, to plead. This was a lesson in real helplessness, and he realized he had never truly experienced desperation before. He had never truly been at the mercy of anyone.

"Please..." he started quietly, feeling a sick bile rise into his throat.

Sassy closed the space between their faces even more. "Shhh... don't beg, Boss. It isn't very flattering for a man to beg."

"Oh, I like it when they beg," Baby drawled in a breathy tone.

Sassy ignored her, bringing the glass to his lips as she used her free arm to prop his head up. The nausea compounded as he felt the slimy liquid against his lips. He pressed them firmly together to try and keep her from pouring it into his mouth, but he detected the slightest salty flavor against the tip of his tongue. He groaned a frantic *huh-uh*, to beg her to stop. The silver lining was that there wasn't much of a smell like he imagined there might be, just the faintest aroma that reminded him of a public swimming pool: chlorine, feet, and wet clothes.

"Open up," Sassy cooed, puckering her own pouty lips in a faux-frown.

He was shaking now, he felt like even his eyelids shivered as moisture pooled at the corners. Tears? Was he crying? Was it just from the urine, or was he really that scared? He couldn't tell anymore. He tried to let himself dissociate as he felt his mouth part open. She smiled, pouring the contents of the shot glass into his mouth.

"There, take it in and swallow..." she instructed.

The snotty globule slid across his tongue in one solid clump, leaving a salty and bitter film. He felt a wave of relief when it was gone, when he'd swallowed it down and felt it disappear beyond the point of sensation... and then he knew he was going to be sick. He heaved involuntarily, regurgitating a wad of vomit. His last meal, long forgotten until now: three fast food sliders, half-chewed fries, and a thick chocolate shake, mixed with the gelatinous semen that he'd barely been able to get down. He was surprised he still had any food at all in his stomach, he felt like he had been here for days already...

"I'm sorry!" Jason slipped before he realized he'd said it, blowing bubbles of saliva and vomit between his lips as he spoke. "I'm sorry..."

"Shhhh... that's alright. Let's just get this all back where it belongs, right?"

"What? What do you mean?" Jason whispered desperately.

Sassy took the shot glass and scooped up the vomit, filling it to the brim.

"Sloppy seconds. Keep it down this time, thirds is going to be even worse."

Jason didn't have time to argue, and he didn't fight her. He wondered why he didn't at least struggle, or attempt to convince her not to do it. His body dissociated, although he could smell and taste the sour aroma of his own void as she poured it into his mouth. It was chunky and thick, with papery pieces that stuck to the roof of his mouth and against his teeth. He swallowed it, gut roaring with disapproval. He talked himself through it slowly.

Breathe, Jace. Breathe. Just take a deep breath, swallow slowly again. Clear your throat, deep breath.

He cleared his throat carefully, feeling the spray of the acid from the pockets of his tonsils, grittiness carried away with what little saliva he could produce.

Sassy leaned in, gently caressing his forehead. "Good boy."

C H A P T E R   S E V E N

Jason didn't remember if he passed out, or if they had knocked him out again. He just knew that he'd been looking into Sassy's eyes and then he was suddenly waking up again. He was chained to the ceiling in the original room again, except now he noted that he was a little lower down. He could plant the balls of his feet more firmly on the floor, allowing him to give his shoulders a much needed rest.

His head throbbed with stress and he was sick to his stomach. They hadn't put any clothes back on him, but at least the room was warm. He imagined it was swelteringly hot outside. It always was this time of year. He was glad, at least, that he didn't have to worry about being cold. It was dark outside, and there was no light source in the room. The only thing that allowed him any visibility at all was what little moonlight came through the window.

Sugarman sat in the same spot he had before, breathing a little noisier than Jason remembered. He knew that he was probably a vegetable, but Jason couldn't help but wish he had some clothes on. He imagined that if Sugarman was trapped inside his mind, but still aware, the last thing he wanted to stare at was Jason's sad dick.

"Hey?" Jason whispered, trying once more to get any kind of reaction at all out of Sugarman. He still didn't move, eyes fixated on the wall beyond Jason, lower lip hanging so heavily that it nearly formed a 'v' below his receded gum lines.

Jason pumped his feet up and down, trying to avoid a cramp in his calf as he bounced to lessen the tension of hanging. "Hey, man. If you can hear me, I just want you to know that I'm going to try to get us out of here. I don't know how… but I'm going to do whatever I can. Just hang in there."

Could a doctor fix Sugarman? Jason doubted that. He looked like he'd had some kind of lobotomy, although he wasn't sure how the two young women could have been able to perform something like that. Maybe it wasn't intentional… maybe an infected head wound or something from one of their torturous sessions.

His mind reeled, ears buzzing so loudly that he almost missed a gentle clicking noise. It was rhythmic, and suddenly it was followed by a mewl. He looked up at the window and saw that a cat was rubbing its body along the glass. With every pass its collar made a little pop against the pane. *A collar.* That meant that the cat had an owner. There were two possibilities that arose from this. Either the cat lived here, or this place wasn't as isolated as it seemed and the cat lived nearby. If he could get that window open, maybe he could scream loud enough that someone would hear him. Or maybe if he could get down, he could somehow put a note on the cat's collar, begging for help.

A scream tore through the room, shaking Jason out of his fantasy plan. The hair rose on his neck, and in the darkness he looked over at Sugarman. He was still sitting there quietly, still. The voice had come from further away, but was undeniably a man's. It ripped through the air again, echoing down the hall and through the bathroom. Whoever it was, they were screaming for their life.

"Please have mercy on me!" the voice screamed.

Jason closed his eyes tightly, pressing them together until he saw bursts of red stars.

"I have a family, please… Dear God, please don't do this. I don't want to die… I don't want—"

The rest was indiscernible. The voice began to babble, sob, moan. The language disappeared, and was replaced by feral screams. A melodious laughter joined his pleas, and Jason knew it was Sassy and Baby. They cackled and giggled like wolves.

And Jason was just thankful it wasn't him.

CHAPTER EIGHT

It was a sleepless night. The man down the hall screamed for most of the night, and the morbid laughter of the girls continued long after he stopped. Jason wondered if he died, or if he had passed out from the pain or stress. Whatever they had been doing to him, he wanted no part of it. He could hear people talking in the house, somewhere. He knew at least Baby and Sassy, but he couldn't figure out if there were more voices, or maybe just a radio or television playing somewhere. He prayed that they were the only two involved in his house of horrors... but *how* could they possibly be getting away with this? With at least three men that Jason knew of?

The door opened and Baby entered. She was cleaned up and, at first, Jason didn't recognize her. She was wearing a pair of high heels, fishnet tights covering her pale skin, and a short white and black polka-dotted dress. Her hair had faint curls and she had fresh makeup on her face. He noticed then that she also had her nails painted a pale pink: carrying a plate and cup in her small hands.

She stopped first beside Sugarman, trying to offer him something fluffy and yellow on a fork, eggs maybe. No surprise, Sugarman didn't react or try to eat any of the food. Jason's mouth watered at the sight of the food and his stomach grumbled. With the wave of hunger, his bladder tightened and he begged it to hold on a little longer.

"You look... really pretty," Jason croaked, voice breaking; his throat was sore from the acid of his vomit.

Baby looked over at him, stifling a smile. "Well, ain't you friendly this mornin'? You can't suck up to me though. I'm still mad at you... but I'll feed ya' a little somethin' before I leave."

Jason watched in agony as Sugarman rejected the eggs. She even scooped a few into his sagging lips, only for them to fall back into the plate in a flood of saliva. She patted his mouth and walked towards Jason with the same plate.

She hesitated. "You know if you kick me or try to fight me at all, you ain't getting away with it, right? You don't wanna be punished again, do ya'?"

Jason shook his head. "No. I won't do anything. I promise."

She continued her approach, stabbing a cloud-like chunk of egg with a fork before raising it to his mouth. Jason found himself pausing, staring at the moist egg as he remembered several pieces had been in Sugarman's mouth. He swallowed back the thought and opened his mouth, allowing her to place a spittle-slick foodstuff on his tongue. Jason found them to have an excellent flavor, when he was able to stop thinking about sharing drool with Sugarman. He couldn't remember the last time he'd had a real scrambled egg. The little pattied egg knock offs were just too easy, and even the 'real egg' at fast food joints just didn't compare to this... drool and all.

"Shugs ain't feeling good," Baby whispered, looking over her shoulder as though she was making sure Sugarman didn't hear her talking about him. "So I'm gonna leave him in here with you, so he don't get lonely. He always hated to be left alone."

"Are you going somewhere?"

Jason asked the question hesitantly, watching her for any sign of anger. If she showed even the slightest spark of irritation, he had a spew of apologies lined up. He was hoping for confirmation that the women occasionally left the house. Any details like this could help him in the future. Especially if they ever let him down from this godforsaken hook.

She furrowed her brows and opened her mouth to speak but he cut her off and said: "You just look pretty, that's all."

"I get dolled up sometimes just because," she said, winking. "Where I'm goin' ain't none of your concern. All you got is time and Sugarman for company. We'll be back."

"What if I have to take a piss?" Jason asked, suddenly reminded of his full bladder.

She laughed, "Well, you just go, silly."

"What if I… you know…" Jason's face flushed. He knew the answer already. Before she even responded he knew that she was going to tell him he had to shit on himself. They'd probably hose the floor down and into the drain.

"Same deal," she confirmed. "Just go."

"I can't go if he's watching."

He was whining. He realized that.

She just laughed as she headed towards the door, "Sugarman sees everything, Boss. Even when he ain't here."

CHAPTER NINE

The daylight wasted away, slowly. Jason endured it for as long as he could and then he allowed himself to go somewhere else. It was interesting how he couldn't remember where his mind took him. He had focused so hard on trying to release his mental anchor to this awareness that he hadn't realized he'd finally drifted until he was coming back. He thought maybe he'd gone back to his childhood, a simpler time. He thought he could still smell breakfast at his mother's house, felt that warm patch on the floor where sun came through the doily curtains, heard the distant drone of the news on the television. Maybe it had been the eggs that triggered the memory.

As night came and lingered on, Jason found himself unable to sleep once again, but this time because Sugarman was wheezing so loudly. He crackled and popped, the wet noise making Jason struggle with his own breath in some kind of subconscious empathy. He tried to block out the sound, he tried to sleep. He couldn't believe how exhausted he was. He'd always been the type to pass out when he got the slightest bit sleepy. Now he was the most exhausted he'd ever been, but hanging here made it impossible to sleep.

Then Sugarman stopped. Jason's head shot up as he realized his wheezing hadn't just stopped... he had stopped breathing altogether.

"Hey, man," Jason croaked. "Hey! Wake up."

After several long seconds, Sugarman took in a long breath. Jason exhaled in relief, head dropping down briefly against his chest.

"Hang in there... Don't leave me here alone."

He felt like he should call him by his name, but using the nickname bestowed upon him by Baby just didn't feel right. It was demeaning, mocking. He wished he knew his real name. Maybe he could call him Bob. Steven. Rodrigo. Literally anything other than

Sugarman. This line of thought led him to another: why did the girls use nicknames if they had no intentions of the men ever getting away? He still held onto the hope that maybe this was some kind of elaborate prank, or some kind of cruel punishment for someone he'd pissed off. If they planned for no witnesses, no survivors, why bother with the nicknames?

He felt hope. Foolish hope, but hope nonetheless.

Jason heard a faint ticking, and his head snapped towards the window where he saw the cat again. He stared back at him for a few minutes, its intense blue-green eyes locking onto his through the foggy glass. It seemed to will him to open the window.

"I can't open the window," he said to the cat. "I wish I could open it, but I can't. I'm tied up, don't you see?"

The cat meowed and began paddling with its front feet against the glass.

"Talking to a fucking cat…" he muttered.

Footsteps sounded down the hall and the door opened, Baby came inside, wearing pajamas. Dressed down as much as she had been dressed up the day before.

"Who you talkin' to?" she asked, eyes moving quickly to Sugarman.

"A cat…" he tried to motion with his head to the window, but when he looked back the cat was gone. The only sign that it had been there at all was the little pawprints left there on the glass.

"A cat?"

"Yeah, is it yours?"

"No, ain't never seen a cat around here. They don't live long outside, on account of the coyotes mostly. Plus, Sassy is allergic, I think."

"Listen, my shoulder is hurting really bad. Really, really bad. I think if I have to hang up here much longer they're going to pull out of socket."

Baby shrugged. "Sassy says your shoulder might already be

MEGAN STOCKTON | 49

dislocated, but we just can't trust ya' enough to let ya' down yet."

"I swear to God I won't try anything," Jason whispered, trying to keep the desperation out of his voice.

"You gotta prove you're a good boy first, Boss. You ain't been nothin' but naughty."

"I think Sugarman is sick," he added quickly. "I think he's really sick."

Baby didn't respond, but she looked down at Sugarman, frowning. Then she leaned down and kissed his cheek before she quickly left the room.

Jason called kitty-kitty the rest of the night, hoping that the little creature would come back. He didn't even like animals, but it was some sign of vibrant life outside of this place.

CHAPTER TEN

At some point Jason had nodded off a little. He woke himself up muttering a rhythmic, "Here kitty… ki'y… kee…"

He gurgled in his chest, coughing once loudly to loosen up the phlegm before he raised his chin from his chest. His eyes felt crusted and they stung with every blink, he would've given anything to be able to reach up and just rub them clean. Sugarman was looking worse, even less responsive with hardly any evidence of life aside from the noisy breaths he took. How did he go so long between each one? Maybe it was the lack of oxygen needed for his brain in this state, Jason didn't know.

The door creaked open and Jason expected to see Baby, but instead Sassy entered. She didn't even look in Jason's direction, walking straight over to where Sugarman sat. She felt his head, pinched his wrist for a pulse, and then she opened her free hand to reveal two pills. She gently, but forcefully, pressed them into Sugarman's mouth. Jason felt himself gag as he watched the entirety of her two fingers disappear into his mouth, shoving the pills beyond his tongue and down his throat. She retracted the saliva-slicked hand, and Sugarman swallowed. He didn't even react, as though he didn't just have damn near an entire arm forced down his throat.

"He needs a doctor," Jason said quietly.

Sassy paused, then looked back over her shoulder at him. She didn't look angry, but more surprised… like she might have forgotten Jason was even there.

He cleared his throat, "He might need a doctor, don't you think so?"

"That's not possible," Sassy responded, standing and wiping the wet hand on her denim shorts.

"You should hear him breathing at night. I think he needs some serious medical help. Professional help. He needs to be *in* a hospital, around-the-clock care. He probably needs IV antibiotics, breathing treatments… Shit, I don't know. I'm not a doctor."

And neither are you. That's what he wanted to say.

Sassy sighed, "Baby is going to be so sad when he's gone. I mean, we knew this time would come eventually… but she is going to be really devastated. Sugarman was the perfect pet."

She paused again, staring at Sugarman for several moments before she whispered, "I won't be around the rest of the day. Shugs isn't going to eat today, so you don't get anything either. Me or Baby will come in to check on you tomorrow."

Jason faltered, watching as she walked away. He wanted to say something to her. Anything to make her stay a little longer so that he could have that engagement. His mind was buzzing with the information she had provided. No food. No company.

"Please," Jason called after her, but Sassy didn't hesitate. If he had any chance at all to convince one of the girls to give him mercy or, best case scenario, to manipulate, it would be Baby.

CHAPTER ELEVEN

Sugarman died that night.

Jason had never seen a man die before. He watched as Sugarman sat bolt upright in the chair, body growing rigid, almost like it was an inflatable being blown up a little at a time. He was taller than he had looked slumped over, and the width of his shoulders when he was sitting up confirmed prior suspicions that once upon a time Sugarman had possessed a little meat on his bones. At first, Jason had been alarmed by the sudden jolt that surged through Sugarman... but then he had realized that he was drawing his last breath.

Sugarman gasped, inhaling until his lungs could expand no more. Then he collapsed onto himself again, letting out a long and rattling groan. He was still, after that point. There was not a twitch of muscle, not a single spasm. He became as inanimate and motionless as the chair he sat in. Even without touching him, Jason knew he was one hundred percent dead.

The only body he had ever seen that wasn't prepared for a funeral was his mother-in-law's. He had always liked his mother-in-law. She was supportive and stayed out of their business, but was still willing to babysit on a whim. Early in the marriage he had been thankful for having in-laws that weren't an issue. She had aggressive colon cancer, and during her last days they stayed in her hospital room in shifts. She had been terrified of being alone. The most capable and confident woman he'd ever known had become this insecure and horrified shell. While so many people in their final days embrace death and come to terms, his mother-in-law never did. He worried about that for a long, long time after she was gone. When she had passed away, Jason had been sitting in the chair next to her. The machines signaled her departure before he ever noticed anything change with her physically. Just like that, she was gone.

He remembered the strange way a body changed after the person had left it. He didn't know if he believed in an afterlife and all of that, but he thought that change was proof enough of a 'soul.'

Sugarman was gone, and Jason was alone. A man was dead, and he was sure he wouldn't be too far behind. This just made everything much more real. This man wasn't an actor; this wasn't a stunt. A person had died, and no one was going to do anything about it.

Urine ran down his own leg and onto the floor. He had initially hated the feeling of his warm piss as it trailed down his skin, but it felt less violating now that Sugarman wasn't there to see it. His skin was raw from the acidic urine drying on him, and his ass cheeks and the back of his balls were even worse from the shit. He had figured as little as he was able to eat and drink, he would have stopped having to piss and shit so much... but he supposed the stress was producing *something* for him to pass all on its own.

Any other time he would have been happy to hear the door to the hallway open. He would have loved for Baby or Sassy to come in and ridicule him so that he had someone to talk to... but when he saw Baby come in with a bowl of oatmeal and a glass of water, his gut instantly sank. He knew that her first stop would be Sugarman, and he knew she would be distraught to discover that he was actually dead.

Instead, Baby didn't even look in Sugarman's direction. She set the glass down on the counter and approached him with the bowl of oatmeal. She rubbed the side of her nose with her thumb and whispered, "Christ, you stink."

The tone of her voice wasn't right. She seemed hateful, aggressive. Jason had always been a little set-off by other people being in a negative mood. He liked to think that it was because he was a kind of empath, but really he just fed off of negativity.

"Can I wash? You can handcuff me or something... but my skin is going to start rotting off... I can't handle the pain, the smell..." Jason glanced longingly at the bathtub under the window. Oh, what he'd give to just soak in a fucking tub for a few hours. He had always thought baths were gross. Marinating in your own warmed-up body stew.... but he'd take it right now. It sounded like heaven.

"I'll have to talk to Sassy... She isn't ready to give you any privileges yet," Baby said, and there was none of that typical mocking humor in her tone. She didn't chide him, or smile. She was as somber faced as Sassy.

"I need more food than this," he added. "I'm so hungry. I don't think I was fed yesterday at all."

"This ain't a continental breakfast, Boss. You get food when we feel like feeding you."

"What's wrong with you?"

There. He said it, and now he couldn't stop. "Is it Sugarman?"

"It's nothin'," she responded, but a blush was creeping onto her cheeks.

"There's still a chance that someone could help him," Jason whispered.

Baby's head shot up, eyes searching desperately. She almost looked like she believed him, like that was the exact kind of hope that she had been hoping for. Jason thrived on that vulnerability.

"We can take him to a hospital. I can drive you there, and you can take him inside… I won't tell anyone what happened. I will just drive away afterwards and we'll never think of each other again. They might be able to help, and you can bring Sugarman back home… where he belongs. With you."

He could see her upset growing, her desperation. He was getting too excited, and he had to resist the urge to push it as far as he could. He had *control* right now. He imagined if she really did let him go. He would suffocate her, just choke her with his bare hands. He didn't care if it took minutes upon minutes… he would choke that bitch for days on end.

"You can help him, Baby."

"Shut up," she whispered.

"You are letting him *die*," Jason barked.

"Shut up!"

"If you leave him here, you are *choosing to let him suffer and die*."

Baby stormed out of the room. She stomped her feet like a little girl throwing a tantrum, and screamed into the hall. Jason screamed back at her, jerking his body around on the restraints angrily. He felt stupid afterwards; it only hurt him, and now his throat felt raw, too. What he didn't expect was for Baby to return so quickly. In less time than it seemed like it had taken her to leave, she was already coming back inside. She left the door standing open behind her, giving Jason his first full glimpse into the hallway. Unfortunately, he wasn't able to take much time to take in any details.

Because Baby had a pair of heavy-duty pruning shears in her hands. It took Jason a minute to figure out what they were: the yellow, rubber-coated handles were longer than her whole torso, her small biceps pushed against the sleeves of her shirt as she came straight for him.

"Hey!" Jason squealed, trying to push himself back away from her. His toes slid around in the mixture of his own shit and piss on the floor, keeping him from getting a good grip on the floor. She lunged at him with the shears, snipping the skin just below his knee cap. She didn't get much meat between the blades, but that didn't matter. It felt like the worst papercut he'd ever had: a burning and stinging that he wanted to blow cool air on to soothe. It was on fire, and his blood felt cool in comparison as it poured down his shin.

"Baby, please!" He was sobbing now. He couldn't control the torrent of tears that poured down his cheeks. "Please, stop. Please."

She circled around behind him and his feet squeaked across the feces-streaked floor, leaving little clean smears like a child's overzealous fingerpainting. He hears the clean *shhhhp* of the blades, and then more pain. At first, he wasn't sure what she'd done. The pain radiated up his entire calf, coming in pulsing waves, the intensity multiplying every time. Then, underneath the overwhelming hurt, he felt the sharp pain against his heel, the sensation of something having popped free. She had cut through his achilles tendon. His leg went to jelly.

"What the fuck is wrong with you?" he cried, trying to look over his shoulder at what she was going to do next. She was trying to get to his other ankle. If she cut that leg too, he had no hope to get away.

He couldn't crawl out of here. He imagined pulling himself along the floor and then down the gravel drive, trying to find the highway through the eyes of a belly-damned serpent.

He swung with his good leg, feeling his aging hip protest with a twinge of pain and a small pop, but he felt his foot collide with her body. He heard the shears clatter to the floor.

"You bad…" Baby growled. She *growled*. "You *terrible man*. You fuckin' piece of shit…"

She moved around his left side, with the leg that was no longer useful to him. She had picked the shears up and held them under her armpit, and reached out with the speed of a viper to grab ahold of his dick. She had a white knuckled grip and he let a shriek escape before he had a chance to stifle it.

"Please, please, please, Baby! Stop! Someone *fucking help me!* Jesus Christ, someone help!"

She opened the shears as wide as they would, sliding it against the base of his shaft, cold metal pressed against his groin. She wiggled the blade and he felt light-headed at the bite of the dull blade on each movement.

"Looks like yer a little big to fit it all in one go, Boss," she snorted, snot running from her pink nose, freckled cheeks blushed red with anger. "I bet you ain't never had nobody tell you that before, huh?"

He then saw something terrifying in her eyes, something a little unhinged. She shrugged her shoulders, putting her arm around the handles. She continued to squeeze his cock in one hand, upper handle crammed under her other arm, free hand on the bottom handle.

"Oh, well. Chomp, chomp," she laughed.

Jason closed his eyes and screamed, preparing for her to effectively cut everything he had off… but then he heard a voice.

"Baby."

Sassy's voice didn't have any urgency or volume, and Jason just barely heard it over his own wails of terror and anticipation. Baby looked over her shoulder, and Jason looked down to see how she shook. She wasn't scared of Sassy, but she was angry that she had been interrupted.

"You know that isn't part of the plan," Sassy said calmly.

"I know it ain't," Baby retorted, snapping. "I know it ain't..."

"Let him go."

"I don't *want* to, Sass. It ain't fair," Baby insisted, voice shaking.

Sassy's calm demeanor didn't falter, but he saw her jaw tense. It was the slightest hardening of her features that suggested she wasn't one to whom you objected.

"Let's go get you in a warm bath, Baby. Hot bath with some bubbles, ice cream on the couch. What do you think?"

Baby looked at Sassy for a few seconds, then back up at Jason. He turned away from her immediately, too afraid that something in his eyes might set her off. He glued his eyes on the far window, listening carefully.

"Fine," Baby whispered, releasing both his dick and the shears at the same time. As the heavy tool fell, it cut the head of his cock on the way down, leaving a gaping gash that bled and dangled. Jason screamed, but it hurt less than anything he had experienced yet. Physically, anyway.

Baby stormed out of the room and down the hall and Sassy stayed glued to the spot, crossing her arms as she looked at Jason. She shook her head.

"I'll be back to take care of what Baby did to you," Sassy said.

"Please don't leave me. Please. Just let me down from here, I won't do anything. I can't fucking do anything. Please," Jason begged.

Sassy didn't show any sign of sympathy, turning her back on him as she headed back out into the hall. "Hang in there, Boss."

C H A P T E R   T W E L V E

The only way Jason could measure time was by watching daylight die and be reborn through the window. That night it stormed for what felt like hours. He wasn't sure. Sometimes seconds here felt like days, and sometimes a day felt like moments. Without the sun, he was lost in a roaring darkness, suffering with his injuries and the fear while he waited on Sassy to come back. When the lightning flashed outside, it illuminated the bathroom in a brief and brilliant blue, intensifying the shadows that were driven to the corners and crevasses. Jason couldn't help but use every opportunity to make sure Sugarman was still sitting where they'd left him.

Sometimes he thought he saw him move, he thought his eyes looked up at him, he thought the corners of his lips turned up at the corners. Sometimes the darkness warped his expression into a cheshire-grin, eyes the size of saucers and glowing chartreuse. Was it the loss of blood? Lack of nourishment? Exhaustion from too little sleep?

Or, alternatively, was it real?

The wind and rain created the perfect environment for him to think he could hear a voice, too. Maybe the voice of Sugarman, maybe the sounds of women moaning, whispering. Sometimes he thought he heard just the end of a tortured scream.

He had never been afraid before. He had never felt fear like this. He was sick with anticipation and anxiety until Sassy finally returned.

She came into the room wearing rubber boots, flipping on a light and setting down a bucket. He looked at her like she was an alien, confused by her sudden appearance in the time warp he'd been in.

"What day is it? What time is it?"

"Eight a.m. on Thursday," Sassy responded dryly.

"You didn't come back…" he found himself whispering.

Sassy shrugged her shoulders, opening a closet somewhere behind him. He heard the door open, but even in the mirror could not see it from his angle. He heard the squeak of water being turned on, and then heard the spray of water from a hose. He watched as the filth beneath him began to come loose and wash away in chunks and slabs, finding its way down the drain in the floor. When she was satisfied with what she had done, she replaced the hose and shut the door, then came over to him with the bucket.

"I had to take care of Baby first," she said, grabbing a clear bottle and popping the top off. "She was very upset. She told me how you antagonized her while she was mourning Sugarman."

"I wasn't antagonizing her—"

"She won't be vouching for mercy for you the next time you're punished. I promise you that."

She turned the bottle upside down, a stream of clear liquid dousing his mutilated cock. It *burned*, it had his entire body alight with pain. The smell reached his nostrils and he realized it was alcohol. She sprayed it onto his knee, then squirted it onto his heel.

"Disinfecting is necessary. Calm down. Do you want your dick to fall off?" Sassy asked.

Jason groaned through gritted teeth as she opened a pack of gauze squares, moistening it with something dark, and then she gently scrubbed away at all of his wounds. He sighed in relief.

"I am so hungry… so thirsty. My shoulders hurt so bad."

"You sound like you think I might care?" Sassy quipped, throwing her dirty gauze into the bucket.

"You can't do this to me."

"I can… and I am."

"Will you at least take him with you?"

"Who?"

Jason nodded towards Sugarman's corpse. He had been surprised at how little it had changed. He had thought that it would bloat and distort. He knew that sometimes bodies moved after death, due to the stiffening muscles... but Sugarman hadn't moved at all. Not other than what he had hallucinated during the storm.

"Him. Sugarman."

Sassy didn't answer him, as usual, and took her bucket as she left the room.

"Please, Sassy. Please take him with you!"

Her pale hand came back into the door, almost like it was a separate entity, and flicked the light off.

CHAPTER THIRTEEN

Jason had experienced a lot of firsts in his life. Most people experienced those same things. First love, first job, first car, first child, first car accident. This place had brought him real fear, real pain, real danger... and now real hunger. He had heard the term 'hunger pains' before, but he had never been hungry enough that it physically hurt like this. It felt like something inside him was gnawing away at his organs, consuming everything around him when it was offered nothing else.

Sugarman now had a mild odor. It came and went, this slightly fruity and sweet aroma. It also smelled like sickness. A bathroom when your kid has had the stomach bug all night, your grandmother's gown at the nursing home, a doctor's waiting area during flu season. He had worried at first that the smell was coming from him, maybe one of his many wounds. He couldn't bear to look down at his dick, the lacerated tip hanging like a crooked hat. Every time he saw it, a nauseating spike of pain shot up his ass.

There was also a bloody froth coming out of Sugarman's nose and mouth, barely visible with only the light from the window. It was bubbling and foamy, like a red frog spawn. The way that it was dynamic with motion made Jason feel like he might have been breathing again. What if he hadn't been dead? What if he was just barely breathing enough for him to see? What if he popped his head up and then jumped up to yell, "Surprise! This was the greatest prank of all time!"

Jason knew better, but his delirium still proposed the idea.

He heard footsteps in the hall, and underneath the gap in the door he saw a shadow approaching.

"Baby?" Jason yelled. "Baby? Is that you? Please come inside."

The shadow paused outside the door, and lingered. He expected whoever it was to just walk away, but to his surprise the door opened and Baby came inside. She was still pissed, he could tell by the look on her face. She somehow looked even younger when she glared at him like that. Before all of this, he would have enjoyed the childish, coy attitude… but now it was a threat of volatility.

She shut the door behind her, but stood with it to her back. She kept her hands behind her too, eyes somewhere between him and the floor.

"I'm sorry, Baby," Jason said. He wanted to sound sincere. If she forgave him, she'd feel sorry for him, and if she felt sorry for him maybe she wouldn't let Sassy hurt him.

"You're only sorry on account of being hurt," Baby responded.

"No, I'm really sorry. I didn't mean to hurt your feelings. It was insensitive of me." He paused, licking his lips. "Hey, you don't have anything you could give me do you? Food?"

She glowered at him. "See? See that? Just apologizin' because you're hungry."

She spun around and he yelled, "Please! Wait! Please, please. I need you, Baby."

With this, Baby paused and Jason took the opportunity to go on, "*I need you.*"

"Nothin' you can say is gonna change anything. You made your bed and now you gotta lay in it."

"What do you mean? What does that mean? Can you at least open the window? Please. To let some of the smell out. It isn't going to hurt anything."

"I really shouldn't do that."

"Please… Please."

Baby seemed to consider what he was asking. Jason thought the fresh air might save his sanity, let a little cool air in and let some of the decaying smell out. He did consider the fact that he had already noticed flies on Sugarman's body, but just a few… with the window open no doubt there would be more. Hopefully he'd be removed before that became an issue though.

She finally walked over and climbed onto the edge of the tub, teetering on her heels as she balanced on the rim. He wished she'd fall. He wished she'd fall and crack open the back of her damned skull. Break her fucking neck, smash her fucking face. He wanted to see her knock her teeth out on the porcelain bath and let them rattle across the floor.

The sound of the window squeaking and sliding open, locking into a position just a few inches higher than it had been before, broke him from his violent desires. He watched as Baby hopped down unscathed, wiping her hands on her thighs.

"There ya go."

Baby left and Jason closed his eyes, imagining that he could draw in that cool air straight to his nostrils and directly down into his lungs. It reinvigorated him, calmed him. He relished the cool breeze and fell fast asleep, more peacefully than he had been the entirety of his captivity.

CHAPTER FOURTEEN

The good night's rest didn't last long.

He heard something making a noise in the middle of the night, and he quickly realized the cat had returned. A lot of good it did him now, still suspended from the ceiling and unable to put a note onto the cat's collar, or to see what address might have been on a tag if the cat had one. Anything to help him know *where* he was would help salvage his sanity.

The cat had one of its little legs stuck underneath the ajar window, swiping its paw in the air as it cried to cram its face under the window. In another circumstance, he might have found the cat's determination charming or comical. Now, he just wanted the cat to go away. There was no real benefit to the animal coming inside, not if it couldn't help him communicate with the outside world.

It managed to squeeze under the window, and plopped onto the floor. It landed with a little spring in its hips. The red cat strode across the concrete floor with the confidence of a runway model. It stretched once, prancing on its front feet and stretching a leg out behind it, tail quivering upright into a curious curl. As it approached Jason, it briefly looked up at him, head swiveling around on its neck as it seemed to try and figure out why he was hanging there in the middle of the floor. It seemed to want to come closer, but instead made a wide berth around the ring of shit and urine staining. Even though Sassy had sprayed the floor down, it was still not clean enough for the cat.

When it realized how boring Jason was in his current state, its interest was diverted to Sugarman. It walked over, rubbing so aggressively against his legs that the wheelchair rolled back and forth a little, making the smallest squeaky sound.

"Hey," Jason scolded. "Hey, leave him alone. Psspssp."

At the sound of the man hissing between his teeth, the cat paused, staring up at him like he had said something incredibly offensive… then it resumed its rubbing against Sugarman's legs before hopping up into his lap. It purred and kneaded his thighs, needle-like claws pricking the fabric that covered his lap. The purring was so loud that it echoed in the room around them. Then the cat turned around to make itself comfortable, as though it would plant itself right there in the dead man's lap to nap the rest of the night…

Except it sniffed Sugarman's nose. The purring stopped. The cat began sniffing so hard that Jason could hear the puffs in and out even at the distance.

"Hey." Jason warned.

The cat's mouth opened…

And it bit off the tip of Sugarman's nose with its little teeth.

"Hey! Knock it off!" Jason yelled, startling himself but leaving the cat unphased as it enthusiastically began chewing pieces of Sugarman's cheek and the rest of his nose. Its ears swiveled excitedly as it tried to decide what to eat next.

"Jesus Christ, psst! Pssst! Stop it! Leave him alone!"

The cat was pleased with this meal, its fat little belly jiggled as it climbed closer to Sugarman's face, kneading little spots on the corpse's shoulders as it continued to consume. It bit into his left eye, chewing aggressively with satisfying smacks and pops. It shook its head once as though offended, sneezing, and slung a shower of maggots onto the floor. They had been embedded behind Sugarman's eyeball and now poured out in a living carpet. They brought with them a new smell: rotten, soured.

Jason closed his eyes, giving up on trying to scare the cat away. It went to a more appetizing area and started eating again.

He fell asleep to the wet chewing and little satisfied growls and purrs of the red cat.

CHAPTER FIFTEEN

Sassy stormed in the next morning startling Jason awake. The first thing he saw was Sugarman's half-eaten face, and he wished he'd thought not to look at him. His cheeks and lips were totally gone: revealing white bone and teeth, one eye socket was totally empty and the other showed a bulging eye that was no longer shielded by a lid. The maggots were gone as far as he could see, and he had a brief moment of panic where he imagined they crawled across the floor as he slept and slithered up his leg into his wounds.

"What the hell is going on in here?" Sassy barked, striding past Sugarman to slam the window shut. "Who the fuck opened this window?"

"I asked Baby to open the window… The smell…"

"You are not *privileged* enough to make any requests around here. Do you understand? Fuck… If Baby has to see Sugarman like this… What the hell happened to him?"

"A cat," Jason explained quietly, calmly. That was when he wondered where the cat had gone. Was it still here? Had it escaped? Was it in the closet? Had it hollowed out Sugarman's guts and climbed inside?

"I fucking hate cats. I'll address this issue with Baby, but for now I'm here to punish *you*. Do you understand?"

Jason's gut sank and he shook his head. "Please."

"You say 'please' a lot, Boss. I don't think that word has the power you think it does… Kind of like 'no,' right? You never took no for an answer, did you?"

"I don't know what you think I did… but you've got the wrong guy. I've never hurt anyone or made anyone do anything they didn't want to do…" Jason insisted.

Sassy rolled her eyes, "Right. Okay, Boss. Here's what's going to happen. I'm going to give you two pills, and you're going to take them. You're going to drink my little sleepy-bye drink, and take a little nap. When you wake up, it'll be your surprise party."

"What if I don't?" Jason asked, trying not to seem defiant. "What if I don't drink it?"

"You're a little stupid aren't you? What kind of teacher are you?"

"How did you know…"

"It's the easy way, or the hard way. If you bypass the easy way, there's no going back. So, what's it going to be?"

They knew he was a teacher. That meant they probably knew his name. He wondered if they'd gotten his driver's license from his wallet and researched him. That also meant they'd have his home address and his family could be in danger. What if they took embarrassing ransom photos of him? Did that even matter?

"Give me the pills," he whispered.

"Thatta' boy." She smiled.

Sassy went to the cabinet and retrieved two powder-blue pills, popping them into his mouth and offering him the straw and cup again. He sucked down the burning liquid faster this time, knowing that nothing made it more palatable or more comfortable. The grogginess came immediately, but lingered. The last time he'd taken the drink, he had passed out much quicker. It was an agonizing wait for the full sedation to take hold. He watched Sassy through blurred vision as she removed Sugarman from the room and brought in another board with straps. He knew that it was for him. His mind tried to come up with all of the terrible things that she might be doing to him, but nothing seemed like it was bad enough.

Slowly, his lids became heavier, and he started blinking more reluctantly. Eventually he could hear Sassy talking to someone, maybe Baby, and then Jason succumbed to sleep.

Jason woke up dizzy. Even before he opened his eyes, he could feel the room swirling around him. His ears were ringing, buzzing with a dull ambience. Something wasn't right with his heart, it fluttered and beat out of rhythm like a moth against a light bulb. More concerning, however, was that he had a massive, throbbing erection. It felt like it was three times the size it should have been, or ever had been.

There was a wet warmth around it, something going up and down: drawing, pulling. *Sucking*. It felt good, but it also hurt. It ached and felt overstimulated. It was too much. How long had this been going on? He opened his eyes and the back of his skull felt heavy as he tried to lift it and look down. There was a scrawny man sucking his dick like he was getting paid. He made direct eye contact with Jason with his jaundiced eyes, intense and refusing to look away. Jason could feel the wounded tip of his penis moving too independently inside the man's mouth. It made him nauseous to imagine a stranger's tongue on the open wound.

Jason tried to sit up, but realized he was strapped down again. Why hadn't he expected that? He felt himself covered in the cold sweat of panic, heart beating even more erratically.

"What the fuck…" he wheezed. "What the fuck…"

Movement in the corner of the room caught his attention and he realized Sassy was standing there, watching. She sauntered over to him, taking her time. She reached down to stroke the other man's blonde hair, winding her fingers affectionately around the curve of his ear.

"You're doing such a good job, Fuzz." She leaned down to coo at him.

"I'm a… good… boy…" he confirmed, mouth still full of dick, slobber and piss-colored precum pouring out the sides of his mouth and down Jason's shaft as he spoke. It pooled on his balls and then oozed down his ass.

"Jason, this is what a good boy does. He listens and does as he's told," Sassy said, "Do you want a chance to show me that *you're* really a good boy too?"

"Yes... Please," he whimpered, sick to his stomach. Every time the man slid his mouth down, the pain had Jason reeling.

"If you cum, I'll let you loose. Not only that, but I won't hang you back up either."

This could have been the simplest request in the world. This would have been the one task that most men would have said they could accomplish. Jason could 'work' under pressure, he wasn't picky, it didn't take much, and he was absolutely a minute man... but this was different. No doubt the pills were responsible for the unnatural, painful erection. The stress of the situation, the crippling anxiety, the man sucking him off...

"I can't," Jason admitted in a whisper.

"What's that?"

"I can't. I won't be able to."

Sassy smiled, leaning down. "You will. If you don't... well, I can think of a few more fun things for us to do with you."

He closed his eyes, breathing slowly through his lips. He tried to think of anyone that he'd rather suck his dick. That wasn't really all that hard... it could've been *anybody*. He thought about Sassy and Baby both, because for some reason he couldn't remember what anyone looked like anymore. He hadn't been here that long, but he was feeling the effects of isolation and neglect. When he imagined his family, they were blurs. He didn't know if he could pick his wife out of a lineup at this point.

A woman's face finally came to mind, probably someone from a porno he'd watched once. In the last couple of years, nothing felt more like home than a nasty porn flick. He liked the movies, something with a little substance. Maybe that was the married man in him. Maybe he wasn't as wild as he thought he was. If he could go back home now, he'd never complain about his sex life again. He struggled to imagine the woman again, holding on to what she looked like. He couldn't picture her entire body altogether, only in chunks. He'd see her face, then a pair of tits, then her ass... Just dismembered body parts floating around in clips like a reel.

Finally, he felt the release... and it sucked. He felt sick. None of the pain subsided, it only intensified. He opened his eyes slowly, looking back down at Fuzz and Sassy.

"Now look how well the two of you are getting along," Sassy said with a smile.

Fuzz looked up at her and whined in his throat, pursing his lips together. Jason realized he was holding his cum in his mouth.

"Oh… hmm… What do you think Jason? Should he swallow or spit?"

Jason was so lightheaded, he wasn't able to formulate a response. He laid with his head pressed back against the board, black dots dancing in his vision.

"No response? My choice then I guess… will you be a good boy and spit it in his mouth?" she asked.

He was alert again, looking down as Fuzz climbed over top of him, hovering over his face. Jason didn't want this. He let himself cry, but he didn't fight. He knew better than that.

He sniffled, opening his lips reluctantly to let Fuzz spit the contents of his mouth into his own. That was also when he realized that Fuzz didn't have any teeth.

CHAPTER SIXTEEN

Sassy did let him go, just like she'd said. She and Fuzz unfastened him from the board and put him into leather wrist cuffs, chaining him to a metal ring on the wall. One hand was directly attached to the anchor, and the other hand was on a chain. There he was given about three or four feet of motion. He was unable to lie down, but he could move the one arm around, he could scratch his shoulder, he could probably sling or push his shit away from him now. It was an improvement. The relief he felt in his joints left him compliant, and he didn't try to escape or fight the pair as he was moved. He found that despite how scrawny Fuzz looked, he was quite strong. No doubt he had been helping Sassy and Baby move Jason when he was passed out. He could've been a swimmer or something, some kind of athlete that was slim but packed with lean muscle.

He had allowed himself to rest again, taking a quick nap. He hadn't been comfortable at first, because Sassy had also left Fuzz in the room with him. Jason was still completely naked, but Fuzz had been allowed a pair of colorful boxers with unicorns and rainbows. Fuzz was wearing a wide collar, and he was hooked to the opposing wall. His hands and feet were free and he could almost reach the center of the floor between them. Jason was jealous of the range of motion and the allowance he was given. But Fuzz was a 'good boy,' and Jason was a bad man.

Baby came in the next morning, seeming a little more chipper. She was more herself, or what Jason perceived to be her normal disposition anyway. She had two paper plates in her hand, a shoulder bag on her arm, and she was glowing with positive energy. She sat down next to Fuzz, who sidled up to her like a dog. She looked in Jason's direction, shoving the paper plate across the floor. The sandwich nearly flew off the plate, and Jason grappled for it so abruptly that he almost toppled.

It was a perfect BLT. He wanted to cry. Looking down at the lightly toasted white bread, cut diagonally and offering him a single triangle, a fresh piece of lettuce, crispy bacon, and a little mayonnaise. It was like seeing the birth of his first child all over again. It was fucking beautiful. Had he ever been this happy? He didn't feel like he'd ever been this happy.

He snatched it up, taking a deep bite that severed the halved sandwich into a quarter. It tasted just as good as it looked. Saliva poured around his teeth and lips and ran down his chin. He closed his eyes, trying to savor the salty, sweet, and sour notes of the sandwich like a food critic. But he could find no faults. He made the mistake of looking up from his sandwich to see her pinching off pieces of the sandwich and hand feeding Fuzz. She would slide the piece of bread into his lips, placing it directly onto his tongue, and he would close his lips around her fingers, sucking off the mayo and grease. Fuzz hummed happily in his throat as she fed him, and the sound reminded him of the hungry ginger cat as it had feasted on Sugarman's body.

Baby noticed him looking and she said, "Sassy says I should apologize to ya', but I don't think I should. I'm glad you got punished again, although I think Sassy took it easy. She said humiliation can be worse than pain."

Jason didn't respond, continuing to eat the sandwich in increasingly smaller bites. When she finished feeding Fuzz, she reached into her pocket and extracted a silver key. Jason sat upright, laying his empty paper plate onto the floor. What was she doing? Baby reached over and unlocked Fuzz's collar. It dropped free from his neck, revealing the mildest pink flesh beneath. He took the opportunity to scratch where it had sat, smiling at her.

Why the fuck didn't he tackle her? Pummel her to the ground? Beat her fucking face in? She was half his size.

Baby put the collar back onto Fuzz's neck and pulled something shiny and black out of the bag she had been carrying. When she first flipped the switch and it started buzzing, Jason thought it might have been some kind of sex toy. But it wasn't… it was an electric razor. Fuzz was hesitant, but bowed his head and allowed her to shave his golden locks down to the scalp, leaving him not just with a buzz-cut, but virtually bald.

Jason was perplexed, but his focus right now was on the lock lying on the floor. Baby had put the collar and chain back onto Fuzz, but she hadn't put the lock on yet. He tried not to let her see him looking at it, instead focusing on her doting for Fuzz. When she was done, she left, and Jason zeroed in on his roommate.

"Hey," he said, leaning as far as he could from the wall and extending a hand. "I'm Jason."

Fuzz looked at him like he was speaking a different language, and he didn't move to try and reach his hand to shake. He just moved over to the wall, leaning back on it.

"Do I know you?" Jason asked. "You kind of look familiar now, without the hair. Where did you work before all of this? Are you from here? Do you know where we are?"

Fuzz looked at him again, rubbing a hand over his scalp, "I don't want to talk about it. I just want to stay alive, and avoid punishment."

"You could have killed her. She let you loose and you have the physical advantage. You could've killed her and gotten the hell out of here. You had a chance last night too, when…"

Jason swallowed back embarrassment.

Fuzz whispered, "You have no idea what they're capable of. You have no idea what they've done to me. What they've done to others."

"There are others?"

Fuzz nodded slowly. "I don't know how many for sure."

"Where did they… get you? Like kidnap you?"

Fuzz looked like his eyes were welling with tears, lips quivering over his empty gums, "I was bad… I did bad, bad things. I don't know how they knew, but they did. I should have never gotten in that car. It was a trap, and I fell for it."

"What did you do? What bad things?"

"What did *you* do?"

"I haven't done anything. I'm a nice guy. I'm a father, a teacher…

I'm a respected member of society."

Fuzz scoffed, "Right. Everyone in here has done something. Sugarman, he…"

His voice trailed off and he looked down, pressing his thumbs together nervously.

Jason kept his voice low and calm, just satisfied that they were getting somewhere. A conversation was soothing to him, even if it was with a brainwashed captive across a nasty-ass bathroom. "Did he talk to you before they… did whatever they did to his head?"

"No… I knew him from before. There were three of us in here that knew each other from before. We…" Fuzz looked up, lips pursing together in what could have been shame. "Kind of worked together."

"Who was the other guy?"

"I don't know where he is. I haven't seen him since the beginning. I'm sure he's dead."

"How long have you been in here?"

Fuzz shrugged.

"Okay listen to me. We're going to work together to get out of here."

"What?" Fuzz suddenly sat up straighter. "Hell, no. You don't drag me into your bad boy bullshit. I am a *good boy*. I will not risk everything I have built with them. They are nice to me and I don't want them to hurt me anymore. They pulled all of my teeth. With pliers. I had to lay there while they chipped them off and broke them into little pieces. They broke my jaw. I couldn't eat. Sassy ran a tube up my nose and down into my belly, and she fed me from a syringe. You don't know what I've been through to make them trust me. No. Hell no."

"Listen to me," Jason said, voice edged with seriousness. "Dammit, *listen to me*. They shaved your head because they're going to fuck your head up like they did Sugarman's. Now that he's gone, Baby wants a new pet and you are a prime candidate, my friend. Why else would she have cut your hair off like that? Huh?"

Fuzz was considering it. Jason could tell that he hadn't thought about the motive behind the haircut. Maybe they wouldn't do that to Fuzz. Jason didn't know. It didn't seem like he was willing to cause any problems, but he would bet that Sassy didn't like to take chances.

"Okay," Fuzz said.

"What?"

"Okay… How do we do this?"

"Baby forgot to lock your collar." He pointed at the lock on the floor. Fuzz looked down at the lock and then up at Jason in surprise, reaching up to rub the naked clasp on the back. "You undo your collar and help me get out of these cuffs over here. Then we'll get into the hall and hopefully find an exit."

"We have to wait until tomorrow. Tomorrow the girls go into town for groceries. We'll have… maybe two hours, tops. More than likely less time than that… but I know where they keep the keys for your cuffs. I can go out, find the key, come back, and we can get out of here."

"Do you know the layout of the house?"

Fuzz wobbled a hand in the air. "Sort of. Sassy doesn't like me to wander around, but sometimes Baby has let me out to walk with her. I know where there's a door… and I think it leads to the outside. That's where they take the dead guys."

Jason took a shaking breath. "Alright. Now all we can do is wait."

CHAPTER SEVENTEEN

Jason had been a little skeptical about Fuzz's awareness of the girls' habits, but the next morning, just like he said, the two women could be heard going down the hallway. When Jason listened very closely, he even heard a door open, and then the voices were more audible outside the window. So at least they knew there was *some* kind of door outside in that direction. Fuzz had grown antsy and anxious the closer it came to making his move. He chewed his short nails nervously, leaving bloody stumps at the end of his fingers.

"Ready?" Jason asked.

"Maybe we should wait a little longer. What if they forgot something and come back inside?"

"You said we had maybe an hour or two, you've gotta get out there now. We don't have time to waste."

"You're right…" Fuzz agreed, reluctant.

He reached up and unfastened his collar, gasping in surprise when it popped off and fell to the floor. Jason gave him a minute to let it sink in, watching as he stared down at the collar and rubbed the back of his neck. Fuzz stood, and it looked unnatural… like an animal standing up on its hind legs. Jason could tell he'd either been crawling or walking hunched over as the shorter women led him on a chain.

He walked over to the door, reaching out to turn the knob. Jason had wondered if it would be locked, although he'd never heard them use a key to get in. It just seemed too easy. Hadn't anyone ever gotten loose before? Why didn't they have some kind of safety measures? Because they were stupid. They were stupid, entitled little bitches. They thought they could just do whatever they wanted to whoever and never have to deal with any kind of ramifications. There were no punishments for what they were doing. Well, if Jason had a chance…

he would absolutely take it. He could think of so many terrible, awful things he would love to do to Sassy and Baby.

In one fluid motion, Fuzz exhaled and jerked the door open, sprinting into the hallway. Jason thought about the possibility that Fuzz would just take the opportunity to escape on his own. To bolt out the door while he had plenty of time to get far, far away. This could be the only opportunity for Jason to ever get free. They were never going to trust him like they did Fuzz, and Jason didn't have it in him to become so docile.

He started counting seconds, moving his finger across the floor to signify each minute that had gone by. He couldn't hear anything, no signs that Fuzz was even still here. It had been at least twenty minutes, if not longer. What was taking so long?

"Fuzz?" Jason called. "You still with me?"

There was no response.

"Fuzz! We gotta get going, man. Ticktock! Losing valuable time here."

Still nothing.

"Fucking dammit…. Fucking *dammit*, he has left me here."

Jason's heart started pounding and he was lightheaded. Maybe he could get far enough away that he could find help and bring them back here. Fuzz didn't strike him as the kind of man who had any survival instincts at all though.

"I'm coming."

He heard Fuzz's voice echo down the hall and he breathed a sigh of relief. He came jogging through the door and started immediately working to unlock Jason's cuffs. He noted that Fuzz smelled good. He was clean and his skin held a lingering aroma of soap that was nearly imperceptible. It was a woman's soap, probably Baby's. She probably gave Fuzz nice baths every week, and he probably was handfed sandwiches like that BLT all the time. The jealousy he felt caught him off guard.

"There you go," Fuzz said. "You're free. Let's go."

"What took you so long?" Jason asked, groaning as he tried to stand. He immediately fell to the floor, clutching his knees in pain. Fuzz hovered over him in concern, but didn't seem to know what to do.

"I couldn't find the key. It wasn't in the dish, but it was in Baby's pocket. I tried the front door... just to see... It's locked somehow from the outside, I guess. There's a lock on the inside, but when you turn it, you still can't get out. I think they have a deadbolt or latch on the outside."

Jason panted through the pain, "We'll bust through it. We have to. The two of us can surely... Ah, fuck. Help me up."

Jason hadn't walked since he had been here. His legs were filled with pins and needless, and hot, angry insects. The writhing, biting sensation gave him goosebumps from the pain. His left leg was still completely fucked. He couldn't walk on it, even flat-footed was going to be hard. He was going to have to rely on Fuzz to help him hobble out of here, and then they were going to have to make tracks as fast as they could away from here.

"Did you see car keys?"

Fuzz hauled Jason to his feet, putting Jason's left arm over his shoulders and hefting him to bear the weight of his injured side. Jason tried not to think about how awkward the skin-to-skin contact was, or how he was completely naked and Fuzz had just sucked his dick a few hours prior.

"Car keys? No, I didn't look for car keys."

"My wife's car is still outside. You can see the bumper from the window. They've got to have the keys in there somewhere. It's going to be really hard for me to run once we're out of here."

I'll just slow you down, let me hide and you go get help. That would have been the responsible thing to say, the kind thing to say. At least one of them would get away, get help, get to safety. But Jason wasn't going to let Fuzz leave him here alone. If Jason didn't get out, neither did Fuzz. If it hadn't been for Jason's encouragement, he would've been fine just being a pet vegetable for the rest of his life. Until he either starved to death or succumbed to pneumonia or whatever the fuck it was that killed Sugarman. Probably aspirated his fucking oatmeal.

"I think I know where they keep the stuff... like the stuff we had with us. Wallets, pictures... *Keys,* maybe. We can check but we've got to go. We've got to go before they get back." Fuzz's voice was shaking, and his body was shaking. He was trembling with fear. He more or less dragged Jason out of the room and down the hallway. Once they were out of the bathroom, he was surprised at how normal the house looked. It had low ceilings, and those wood panel walls and carpet could've been in any fifty-year old-trailer. It was nothing terrifying, nothing out of the ordinary at all.

They went into a main kitchen and living area, and Jason saw the front door to their left. It was tempting to just go ahead and try to get it open, to try to get out, but he reminded himself that he was in no shape to flee on foot. Fuzz took them to the right, past the brown floral couch and tube TV, down another small hallway. There were what looked like clothes on the floor halfway down: a bunch of shirts and dirty shorts, maybe pieces of cut-off fabric. Jason thought that he recognized some of his clothes he was wearing the day of his abduction.

Fuzz leaned him against the wall, stabilizing him before letting go.

"That down there is where they put all the stuff, I think. Baby told me I'm not allowed to even step foot down that hallway, she said I'd regret it... said she'd know if I went down it, even if she wasn't looking." All color drained from Fuzz's face as he stared down the hall, Adam's apple bobbing nervously.

"Just check for the keys... Just a real quick in and out. Nobody is gonna know you tried to go down there. You don't belong to those cunts, we're going to send them to prison for the rest of their lives. Put them under the prison if we can."

"Right. Send them to prison," Fuzz repeated, voice still lacking any confidence. He wiped his sweaty hands on his bare thighs and headed down the hallway. He walked with a painstakingly slow pace, creeping down as though he were afraid someone might pop out at any moment.

Fuzz was halfway down the hall now, and he pushed the clothes out of his way with the top of his toes.

"Those are my pants!" Jason said quickly. "Check the pocket first."

Fuzz turned around to look at him and nodded, seeming relieved to have any excuse not to head on down to the door yet. He crouched down, sifting through the clothes. Then he screamed. Jason was so startled that he fell to the ground, adding his own cries as pain coursed through his left calf. Fuzz was howling. A yelp that had started as a high-pitched wail and then droned off into a throaty moan.

"What the fuck! No, no, no, no!" Fuzz screamed, kicking the wall hard enough that the structure of the home seemed to shake and echo around them.

"What happened?" Jason screamed, dragging himself down the hallways towards Fuzz. "Talk to me, what is it?"

"I'm dead. They're going to kill me. I am dead."

Fuzz was sobbing. When Jason finally got close enough to him he had snot, tears, and saliva pouring down his face in a flood of liquid. Jason was stunned. He felt cold all over, his mind immediately went distant and dim.

There was blood everywhere. It was splattered on the walls, pooling in the floor, soaking the clothes. At first it looked like the clothes had turned into a creature, reaching up to grab him with their deceptively soft-looking mouth… But then he saw the shining metal beneath.

A bear trap. They had set this trap here so that if someone stepped on or scooted the clothes with their feet, they would be caught. Except Fuzz had reached down with his hand. His wrist was smashed backwards somehow, the back of his hand laying flush with his forearm. His fingers were a crooked, tangled mess like a bundle of necklaces tossed into a box. Jason started to reach down and try to pry the trap open, but then he was overtaken by the fear that more traps may be hiding beneath.

"Can you pull the trap up?" Jason asked. "Is it attached to the floor? Try to pull it up."

"I can't…" Fuzz cried, voice cracking. "I'm gonna die…"

Jason reached over, grabbing Fuzz by the elbow and pulled him forcefully. The trap briefly lifted, but then they reached the end of an anchor and the sudden resistance caused Fuzz to scream even louder.

"Push the clothes out of the way." Jason demanded.

"What?"

"Use your other hand to push the clothes out of the way. I'll go try to find the key and I'll rip that trap up out of the floor. I can't jump over or step over the pile, not with my bad leg… Just clear me a path."

"I'm scared."

"Don't be a fucking pussy." Jason snapped. "Do it or I'll leave you here for them to find. I'll go lock myself back up in the bathroom and they'll see how bad you've been. Is that what you want?"

Fuzz shrank into himself, terror on his face compounded by this betrayal. The regret and the despair were palpable. He whined in his throat, moving forward, to push the clothes out of the way with shaking fingertips.

"That's it…" Jason encouraged, sweat forming on his own brow. "Little faster, we don't have much time."

Then he heard it again. It happened so fast. Another trap. This one was without teeth: just two flat, dull pieces of metal that clamped shut. It looked like it leapt up from the pile of clothes, lunging for him. There was no blood this time, but where it made contact immediately bruised. It was black, pregnant with blood from damaged capillaries.

Fuzz released a feral yowl, babbling unintelligibly. Jason stared down at his two trapped hands, and then at the door beyond. He was trying to come up with a plan, a way that he could get to that door without being caught in a trap as well, if any remained.

But Jason didn't have to think about it for very long.

Behind him, the front door was being unlocked. Fuzz heard it too, and he tried to reach towards Jason with his hands, only hurting himself further in the process.

"Don't leave me," he cried, blowing bubbles from both his lips and nostrils. "Please don't let them hurt me again. Please."

Jason turned away from Fuzz, and didn't look back as he started crawling on his hands on one knee as fast as he could. The door opened and Baby stared down at him from across the room, eyes wide. She had a single jug of milk in her hands, and when she looked beyond Jason and saw Fuzz in the hallway, she dropped the jug, gasping, and covered her mouth. Sassy was right behind her, pushing past to see what was going on. She laid down several bags of groceries.

"Baby, get the juice."

Baby darted across the room, slinging a cabinet open and pulling out a glass amber bottle with a piece of tape across the front that read JUICE in sharpie. She dumped it on a rag and started towards Jason. This was his chance. He stood on his single knee, prepared to fight her. If he could get ahold of her, he could do serious damage. She was weak. He wasn't a gym rat or anything, and he wasn't in his prime anymore, but he was a man and she was a little girl.

That wasn't Jason's experience though. Sassy tackled him to the ground, yanking his arm around behind, twisting it. He could feel his shoulders grinding, muscles and ligaments screaming against the torque. Baby clamped the rag over his mouth and nose, shoving his head onto the ground. He gasped, struggling to breathe in the fumes created by the mystery liquid. The *zzzzp* and sudden tension on his wrists led him to suspect he had been zip tied.

His body was heavy and he was down. They let him rest on the ground, head swimming. He was facing the hallway, where he could see Fuzz watching the scene unfold. Sassy picked up a hammer from the kitchen table and the two of them approached Fuzz side-by-side. He could barely see them at the distance, silhouettes. The hammer had a spike on one end, he noticed. Sharper and longer than a regular hammer. He could see Fuzz... he could see his face as clear as day.

"No, no, no, no..." Fuzz cried. "Baby? He made me do it, Baby. I knew he was bad and it was a bad idea. I knew it was."

Sassy and Baby exchanged silent glances, and didn't say anything.

"I'm a good boy..." Fuzz cooed at her, leaning his head in as though he wanted her to scratch it.

Baby put her hand out, and Sassy put the handle of the hammer in her hand.

Baby planted her feet, and in one swift swing, Fuzz was dead.

C H A P T E R   E I G H T E E N

Jason's awakening was rocky, like he was suffering from a really gnarly hangover. His head hurt, his body hurt. How many times could you do that to someone before it started causing side effects? Before it started causing irreversible damage? At this point, Jason didn't even know if he'd live to have to worry about anything long term. He could die here. Just like Sugarman. Just like Fuzz.

He thought he might feel guilty about Fuzz's death, but he found that he really didn't care. Fuzz had a lot of opportunities to escape before Jason had come along, and he hadn't taken them. Fuzz was a *victim*. He had probably always been a victim. He probably walked right in this torture chamber and signed a contract.

"Hey, Boss."

Sassy's voice brought him out of his thoughts and he opened his eyes slowly. She was standing in front of him, bent over with her hands between her knees. She smiled at him, and he didn't think she'd ever *really* smiled. It scared him. He went on the defensive. He was handcuffed now, he thought. He wiggled his wrists around behind his back, feeling cold metal and a chain between. His legs were free, he wasn't attached to the wall. With only one good leg, though, he didn't think he could get out of here regardless. He definitely couldn't fight Sassy. Not unless he could get his hands around in front of him somehow.

"It's time for you to play the game."

She moved a chair near him, sitting down and crossing one leg over the other. She took a deep breath, and he knew she was about to tell him something either very important to her, or very important for him.

"Sassy isn't my real name, I'm guessing you knew that, but it doesn't really matter what my real name is because you don't know me… But I know you. Almost twenty years ago my mother was molested in school by one of her teachers. That teacher was you."

Jason's jaw dropped. "I have *never…*"

"I'm going to ask you once to not interrupt me," Sassy snapped. "If you interrupt me again, I will cut off your tongue and shove it up your ass, am I abundantly clear?"

Jason nodded slowly.

"My mother was molested *by you.* She tried to tell someone what had happened, but no one believed her. Not a soul. She ended up getting pregnant and dropping out of high school, and years later… Baby's mom was molested by the same man in the same school. *By you.* Baby's mom also tried to tell someone, anyone really. She told the principal, she told her homeroom teacher, she told her parents… No one believed her. No one except… my mother."

Sassy paused, giving him a second to let everything soak in. He wanted to ask Sassy who her mother was, who her father was. Was it possible that *he* was her father? Did that timeline add up? No. He had always worn a rubber if he ever actually penetrated the girls, but mostly he pressured them into oral or anal… much safer all around. He had spaced out all of these events, how did two girls find each other? He had too many questions.

"You see, my mom went on to get her GED and eventually she started working at a youth center. That's where she met Baby's mom. But Baby's mom couldn't cope. She couldn't handle no one believing her, and I mean… don't take all of the credit, she was also a single mom and on some hardcore drugs. So she killed herself, and that left Baby to fall into the foster care system at a young age." She paused again and Jason hesitantly asked, "And what about Sugarman? What about Fuzz? If you're trying to play this like it's personal against me… Like you think whatever you're accusing me of is worth this torture, this absolute insanity…"

Sassy quirked a brow. "I think the most insane thing about this entire situation is the fact that you don't think you deserve this. That you don't deserve *more* than this. Do you believe in Hell? I don't, but Baby does. I want to make sure that, just in case there's nothing after this life, you suffered. I want you to feel it all. I want you to start to regret what you did to our mothers, to other girls. I want you to realize what you are. You're a fucking disgusting piece of human garbage. You are shit. You are a disgusting pervert, pedophile. You're a bad man."

Jason's face was hot. He wasn't sure that he realized how passionately people felt about this. They hadn't been *children*, they'd been *teenagers*. Wasn't there a difference? Wasn't that some kind of taboo gray area? Was he fucked up? Broken somewhere in his head? Or had he been so desperate for sex, control, and power that he didn't care who he hurt?

"What did they do then?" Jason asked again, clearing his throat. "I thought they were *good boys*."

"Sugarman was a CPS officer, when Baby was in the system, he sold her for sex to two guys that worked at the police department. Whole corrupted fucking system... Baby didn't deserve that. Have you seen how she lights up a room? Baby is pure and good, and Baby *loves*." Sassy lingered there, staring at the floor between them. Then she put her hands together and leaned back into her chair as she went on, "So when Baby was phasing out of the system we reconnected. My mom died in a car accident, and neither of us had anybody. We started talking about all of the people who had done us wrong... all of the men... and then all of the people who had enabled them and protected them. We can't get 'em all, Boss. We know that. It won't always be just the two of us though, there are a lot of girls out there just like us. But back to Sugarman... He tried to fight us one day and we hit him in the back of the head. Just *pop*, one good whack to the back of his skull. It cut through the meat and bone and everything. Piece of his brain came out like a kabob. We thought he'd be dead for sure, but then when he came back to us, he was... well, you saw him. It was something for Baby to take care of. She likes pets, projects. She's a little rough on real animals, she's got a temper sometimes you see. A little feisty. But a grown man can take all the abuse he puts out. So we kept ol' Sugarman around."

"And the two cops? Just gonna let them go?"

"Nah, one of them's long since dead. He couldn't hack it. Had to put him down pretty early on, but we had plenty of fun with him. One of my favorite playthings. Then there's Fuzz…"

Jason looked up at her, and she smiled.

"Oh, you're surprised? Why do you think Baby called him Fuzz? He was this young, rookie cop. The other guy, Baby called him Porky, was his senior officer. Fuzz just went along with anything. He was soft. He was a follower. Porky was getting his dick wet, and Fuzz wanted to as well. Fuzz ended up being pretty easy."

"What's this game?" Jason asked, realizing too late that he had cut her off. She didn't look at him with the same anger as before. Instead, she looked like she might have been glad that he finally asked. He wanted to ask more questions. What were the rules? What were the stakes?

"Well, I haven't been completely honest with you, I guess," Sassy admitted. "Calling it a game makes it sound like there's teams and sides… Or that you're actually playing. That you actually have a chance to 'win.' This is really just for someone else. So I'm going to give you one chance to come completely clean with me. Do you have anything you want to confess? Anything you want to admit that you've done?

Jason didn't speak. He thought that if he gave in, it would add some kind of finality. He looked away from her and she took a long inhale.

"Well, I'll confess to you then. I'm the one that lured you to the motel that night. It was so easy. I literally took one of the top search results from online and put on that fake profile. I had planned on going to pursue you the next day but I didn't have to… you came straight for me. Baby was bait, of course. You didn't have to pick her up. You didn't have to take the bait. I would've been waiting at the hotel anyway. It wouldn't have mattered in the end, I guess."

There was a knock on the door and Sassy looked up. "Well, that's all the time we have."

"What are you going to do to me?" Jason asked, desperate. "We're not done talking. I have questions."

"Oh, I'm not going to do anything to you. I wouldn't want to strip that honor from her."

"From who?"

Sassy walked over to the door and put her hand on the knob. She looked over her shoulder at him once, smiling again.

"Who is it, Sassy?" Jason screamed.

She pulled the door open, and on the other side stood a teenage girl. She was holding a machete in her hand. She didn't look nervous, but excited. As soon as the door parted enough to allow light onto her face, he recognized her as one of his daughter's ex-friends. A girl that he *had* at one point maybe propositioned, but she hadn't turned him down. Not really. She might have said she didn't want to, but she didn't try to stop him. She had a falling out with his daughter not long after that, and he'd never had to worry about her again.

But here she was.

She smiled at him, tucking her dark hair behind her ear. "Hello, Mr. Burnham."

ABOUT THE AUTHOR

Megan Stockton is an indie author who lives in Grimsley Tennessee with her two children and her husband, who is an indie filmmaker. She writes in a variety of genres that all have dark/horror elements, and all of her work is character-driven and immersive. She is known for delivering works that are raw, thought-provoking, brutal, and cinematic. She has been writing since she was a child and was always obsessed with horror and the macabre. When she isn't writing (or working her day job) she likes to work with the animals on their farm, read, play video games, and watch movies.

ABOUT THE
PUBLISHER / EDITOR

Dawn Shea is an author and half of the publishing team over at D&T Publishing. She lives with her family in Mississippi. Always an avid horror lover, she has moved forward with her dreams of writing and publishing those things she loves so much.

Follow her author page on Amazon for all publications she is featured in.

Follow D&T Publishing at their website, **www.dt-publishing.com**, or search for their Facebook Group

Or email here: dandtpublishing20@gmail.com

Impulse by Megan Stockton

Cover art by Don Noble

Edited by Tasha Schiedel

Formatted by Ash Ericmore

Made in United States
Orlando, FL
05 April 2025